DO ANIMALS DREAM?

DO ANIMALS DREAM?

Children's questions about animals
most often asked of
The Natural History Museum
answered by Joyce Pope

Viking Kestrel

VIKING KESTREL
Viking Penguin Inc.,
40 West 23rd Street, New York,
New York 10010, U.S.A.
Penguin Books Canada Limited,
2801 John Street, Markham, Ontario,
Canada L3R 1B4

Conceived, edited and designed by
Marshall Editions Limited
170 Piccadilly
London W1V 9DD

Artists
Richard Orr
Michael Woods
Editor
Jinny Johnson
Art Editor
Mel Petersen
Art Assistant
Arthur Brown
Managing Editor
Ruth Binney
Production
Barry Baker
Janice Storr

First published in 1986 by Viking Penguin Inc.
Published simultaneously in Canada
Printed in Portugal by Printer Portuguesa

2 3 4 5 90 89 88 87

Library of Congress catalog card number: 86-40029
(CIP data available)

ISBN 0-670-81233-1

Contents

1

How many kinds of animal are there?

Well over a million different kinds of animal are alive in the world today, but, since new ones are regularly discovered, nobody knows the exact total. It is unlikely that there is another kind of giraffe or elephant, so all the big creatures are probably known. Yet, a new kind of bat, the hog-nosed bat, was found in 1973 and almost every year several new kinds of bird are identified.

Kinds of animals are more correctly termed species. A species is a group of animals that can, in principle, breed successfully with one another. Members of the same species share the same basic characteristics, with minor variations between individuals.

The animal world is divided into two major groups—invertebrates and vertebrates. Invertebrates, animals without backbones, include creatures such as insects, worms, spiders, crabs, limpets and the many kinds of virtually invisible creature. Animals with backbones, vertebrates, include the more familiar fish, reptiles, birds and mammals.

Tiny insects dominate the animal world. There are more species of insect than of all the fish, amphibians, reptiles, birds and mammals put together, and many more are yet to be discovered and named.

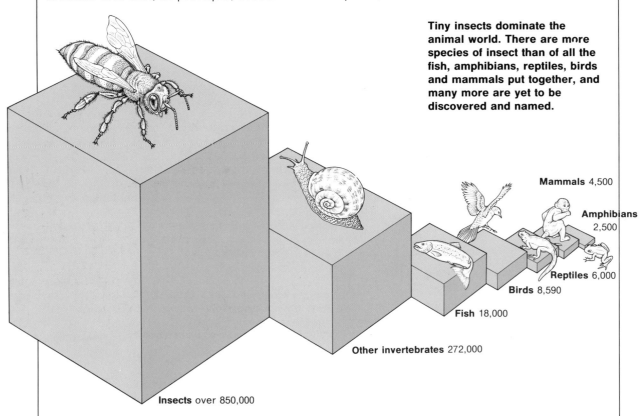

Mammals 4,500

Amphibians 2,500

Reptiles 6,000

Birds 8,590

Fish 18,000

Other invertebrates 272,000

Insects over 850,000

2

Why are some animals so rare?

An animal species may be rare because it lives in an isolated area, such as an island or lake, from which it cannot escape to spread its kind. Island creatures such as the Aldabra brush warbler and many species of Hawaiian honeycreepers are among the rarest of all animals, with populations so low—under two dozen for the warbler—that they are in danger of becoming extinct.

Other creatures are uncommon because they feed solely on plants which grow only in one area, or because they need to have particular conditions of climate that occur only in a restricted area.

A species can gradually become extinct as a result of natural "disasters," but many more are in danger because man has killed too many of them or destroyed their living places. Even common creatures can be affected in this way. The passenger pigeon, once the most abundant bird in the world, was totally exterminated by hunting and by destruction of its forest home. Today many more creatures, such as rhinos, elephants and whales, are dangerously rare for much the same reasons.

The giant panda, symbol of the World Wildlife Fund, is famous for its rarity. Its numbers have certainly dwindled to less than 1,000 and possibly even to less than 500 in the wild. Pandas are now found only in the mountains of southern China, but in prehistoric times probably lived in other areas of China as well. One reason for the panda's rarity is its diet. It feeds mainly on bamboos, which periodically die out over huge areas, leaving the pandas with no food supplies.

Giant panda

3

What is the difference between crocodiles and alligators?

Alligator

Crocodile

The crocodile has a long snout with strong teeth, one of which always remains showing when the animal closes its mouth. The alligator typically has a broad snout but no teeth show when its mouth is closed.

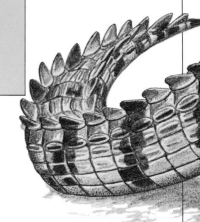

Crocodiles and alligators do look similar—they are closely related and have much the same way of life. Crocodiles live in all tropical parts of the world, but all alligators, apart from the rare Chinese alligator, live in North or South America. The gharial, also known as the gavial, is a rare crocodilelike animal which lives in India.

4

Do crocodiles cry?

Crocodiles' eyes produce tears just as ours do, and crocodiles are sometimes seen with dark streaks of water dribbling down their faces, probably caused by tears. Nobody knows exactly why this should happen but the tears may be a means of getting rid of excess salt from the crocodile's body.

People once thought that crocodiles attracted prey by pretending to weep and moan and then ate up anybody or anything who came to see what was the matter. This legend is the origin of the saying "crocodile tears," meaning tears which are not ones of genuine pain. It is, of course, untrue.

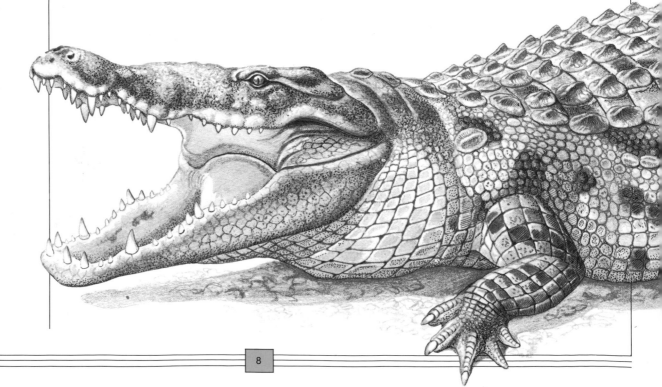

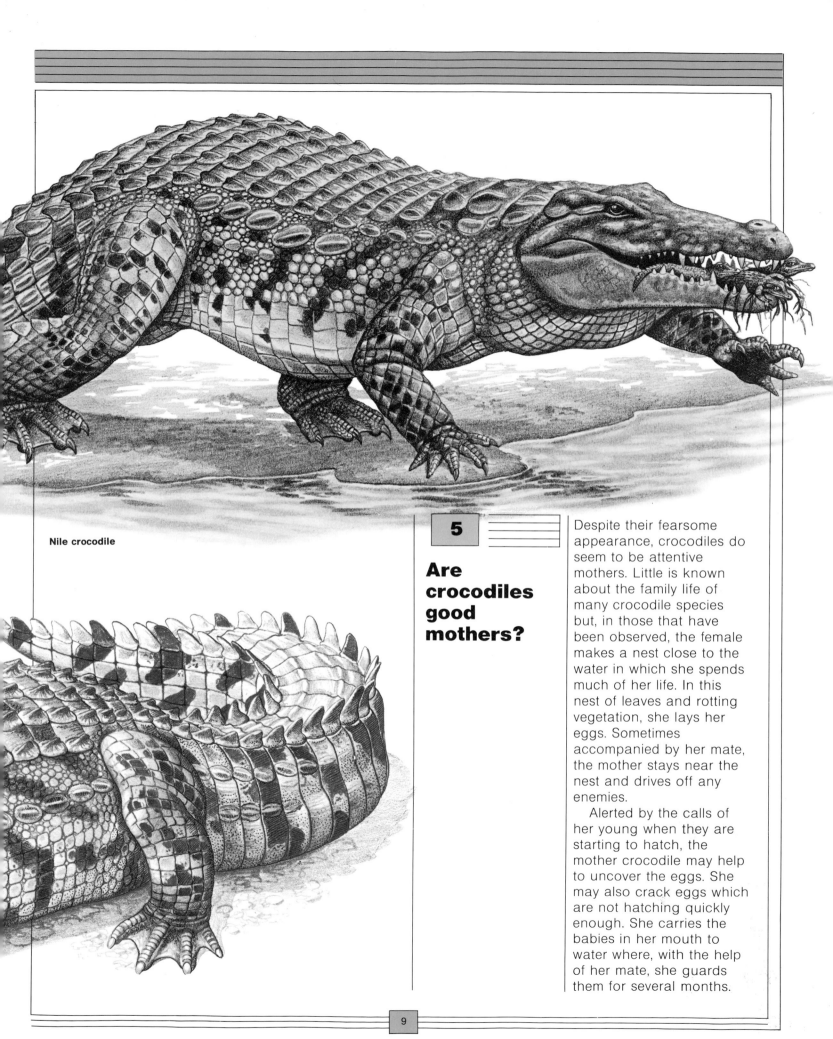

Nile crocodile

Are crocodiles good mothers?

Despite their fearsome appearance, crocodiles do seem to be attentive mothers. Little is known about the family life of many crocodile species but, in those that have been observed, the female makes a nest close to the water in which she spends much of her life. In this nest of leaves and rotting vegetation, she lays her eggs. Sometimes accompanied by her mate, the mother stays near the nest and drives off any enemies.

Alerted by the calls of her young when they are starting to hatch, the mother crocodile may help to uncover the eggs. She may also crack eggs which are not hatching quickly enough. She carries the babies in her mouth to water where, with the help of her mate, she guards them for several months.

6

What is a prehensile tail?

Spider monkey

A prehensile tail is one that can grip.
Human hands, too, are prehensile—the
word simply means "able to grasp." Some
forest-living animals have one of these
specialized tails which they use as a fifth
hand for holding onto branches as they
travel through the trees.

Like many South American monkeys,
the spider monkey has a prehensile tail. A
powerful yet flexible structure of bone and
muscle, the tail is strong enough to
support its owner's full weight, leaving the
hands free for finding food.

Do animals other than South American monkeys have prehensile tails?

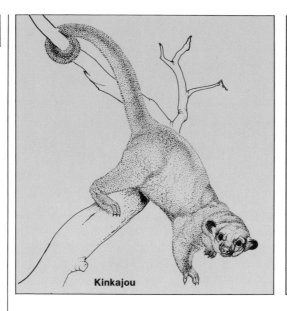
Kinkajou

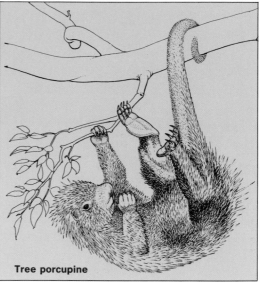
Tree porcupine

Tree pangolins and porcupines, an anteater, many rodents, some pouched relatives of the kangaroos, and the kinkajou, a cousin of the raccoon, have prehensile tails. All are tree-dwellers and find an "extra hand" extremely useful as they climb.

The fruit-eating kinkajou can hang from one branch of a tree by its tail while it picks fruit on another with its hands. For the slow-moving porcupine the tight grip of its tail is also a protective device—predators find it hard to dislodge.

How do tree-living animals manage without prehensile tails?

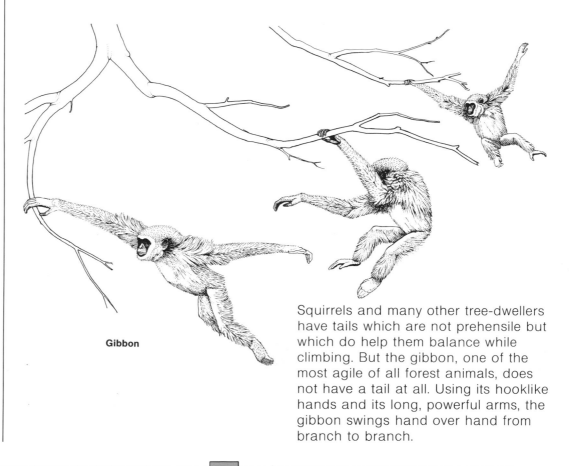
Gibbon

Squirrels and many other tree-dwellers have tails which are not prehensile but which do help them balance while climbing. But the gibbon, one of the most agile of all forest animals, does not have a tail at all. Using its hooklike hands and its long, powerful arms, the gibbon swings hand over hand from branch to branch.

Are bats really blind?

No normal healthy bat is blind. Indeed, some, such as the fruit bats, have large eyes and reasonably good sight. These, combined with their excellent sense of smell, help them find the fruit on which they feed.

Most bats, though, have small eyes and poor sight. They are active at night, when vision is least useful, and their eyes tend to be widely spaced on either side of the face, making it impossible for them to be able to judge distances well enough to catch prey by sight. Since many kinds of bat eat insects, hunt other small prey or catch fish, they must have a means of locating prey apart from sight. Even bats which have been blinded catch their food with ease.

The large and complex ears possessed by most bats provide a clue—bats find their prey or detect the presence of obstacles in their path by means of animal sonar. This is the use of sound waves for detecting objects in the dark.

As it flies, the bat gives off a series of high-pitched squeaks, far above the level of hearing of human ears. These sound pulses bounce off any prey or object in their path and return echoes to the bat, providing information as to the type of object, its position, speed and direction of movement. By analyzing these sounds, the bat can pinpoint the exact location of the object and home in on it.

Some species, such as the horseshoe bats, have complex nostrils through which they hum their sound pulses. Others have simple noses and emit their squeaks through open mouths.

The hunting bat gives out high-pitched sounds as it flies through the darkness. If the sound pulses meet an object moving away from the bat, the note of the returning echo drops. If it meets an object, such as a moth, moving toward the bat, the note rises. The degree of the change depends on the speed of the object. As echoes bounce back, the bat responds by stepping up its rate of sound production. In the closing phase of an insect hunt the bat may emit more than 300 squeaks a second.

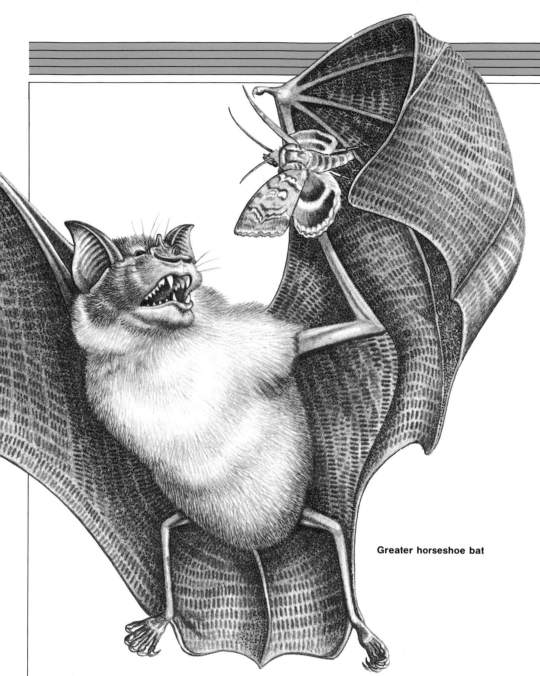

Once the horseshoe bat has found its prey by means of sonar, it may seize the meal in its mouth or scoop it up in its wing. The prey is then carried back to the bat's roost.

Greater horseshoe bat

10

Do any other animals use sonar?

Two kinds of bird use sonar—the oil birds of South America and several Southeast Asian species of cave-roosting swiftlet. Unlike bats, these birds make low- rather than high-pitched clicks of sound but use the clues that the echoes provide in a similar way to locate their prey.

Sound travels well through water and many species of dolphin and whale use sonar to detect prey. Like bats, whales and dolphins use bursts of high-pitched sound.

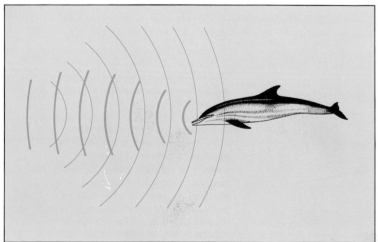

Tests on captive dolphins show that they can distinguish between different kinds of fish by means of sonar.

11

Why are male animals often larger and more showy than females?

The reasons why male animals differ from females are nearly all connected with finding a mate. Colorful or highly ornate male animals, such as the peacock, usually belong to species where the female chooses her mate from males who show themselves off by posturing or dancing. The brighter the male, the more likely he is to attract a mate. In these species, beauty ensures breeding success.

Male animals which are noticeably larger than their females, or which have weapons such as horns or antlers, usually have to fight rivals to win a territory and a mate. Superior male strength also helps them maintain their territory and protect their mate and offspring.

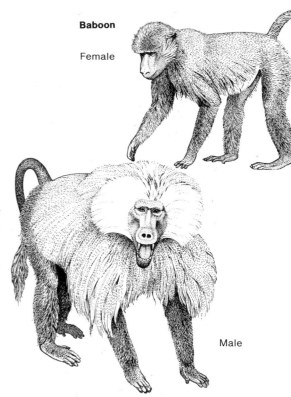

Baboon

Female

Male

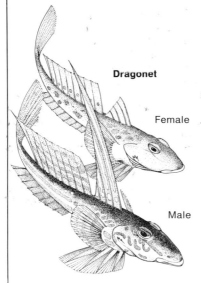

Dragonet

Female

Male

The male dragonet fish is larger than the female and has an extra-long fin on his back. He is also brighter in color than the mainly brownish female, particularly around the head and fins. To attract a mate, the male dragonets dance in front of females, displaying their bright colors and long fins until the females make their choice.

At as much as 66 lb (30 kg), male baboons are twice the weight of females and have thick manes which make them look even bigger than they are. Huge canine teeth are formidable weapons. The impressive appearance of adult males intimidates enemies such as lions and hunting dogs and so helps protect the troop.

The male peacock spreads the gorgeous plumes of his upper tail coverts—the feathers that cover his real tail—and parades in front of his drab mate. Like most birds in which the male is brilliantly colored and the female is not, the peacock does not stay with one hen. He attracts as many females as possible and, after mating, leaves them to make the nests, incubate the eggs and look after the baby birds alone.

Young male peacocks resemble females, only developing their splendid feathers when fully adult.

Female

Peacock

Male

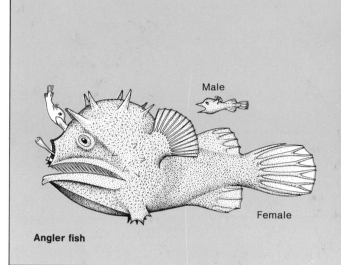

The males of some deep-sea angler fish are only about 2½ in (6 cm) long when fully grown, while their mates may be as much as 3 ft (90 cm). These anglers live in the sparsely inhabited ocean depths down to 3,000 ft (900 m), where mates are hard to find. When a male does meet a female he hangs onto her and eventually becomes a parasite, nourished directly from her blood system. He is then always on hand to fertilize the female's eggs.

Male

Female

Angler fish

Glow-worm

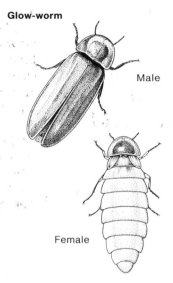

Male

Female

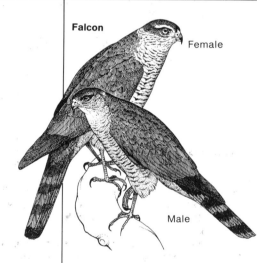

Falcon

Female

Male

Female birds of prey are as much as 30 percent larger than their mates. This difference is thought to reduce the risk of fighting in the early stages of courtship—birds more nearly matched in size would be likely to see one another as rivals for a territory.

Because of her size the female may feed on larger prey than the male. The pair can then make more efficient use of a smaller territory than if both were chasing the same prey.

The glow-worm—which is not a worm at all but a beetle—gives off greenish light from glands near its tail. To attract a mate, the wingless female simply reveals her light. The keen-sighted, winged male soon spots the glowing female and flies to her.

Male deer are easily identified by the branched bony growths, antlers, on their heads. In the breeding season, or rut, rival males fight by locking antlers and pushing until the weaker is overcome. The winner mates with the females in the group. Each year the antlers are lost and regrown and as the animal matures, each set becomes larger and more complex than the last. This difference prevents fights between animals of different ages that are not well matched.

Antlers are also used to spread scent from facial glands over vegetation in a deer's territory. The scent warns off rivals and attracts females.

Fallow deer

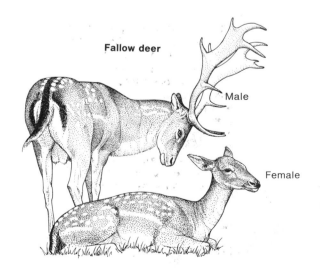

Male

Female

Do all birds sing?

Sedge warbler

Californian white-crowned sparrow

All birds have voices, but only some birds sing. Gulls, grouse and woodpeckers, for example, make a variety of sounds which tell their neighbors of fear, threat or the presence of food. These sounds do not have to be learned—they form an inborn part of the birds' behavior.

A large group of birds, the passerines, or perching birds, can make a much wider range of sounds. These are the songs so admired by humans. Mainly performed by the males, the songs include information calls but these are combined with elaborate trills which may vary from one individual to another. The pattern of the song is the same within any one species.

Such songs are important to birds for defining and defending territory and also serve to attract females. A bird must learn its song from another male bird, first from its father and later, during its first breeding season, from its neighbors.

Birds usually sing from a prominent perch but, in open country, may perform a special song flight. Beautiful songs do not necessarily go with beautiful birds. Some of the most elaborate songs are produced by drab birds such as the sedge warblers.

Detailed studies of the Californian white-crowned sparrow have shown that different populations of the birds have slightly different versions, local dialects as it were, of the species song.

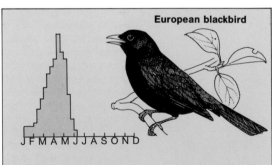

European blackbird

J F M A M J J A S O N D

Most birds sing only when they are setting up territory and looking for a mate. Once these tasks are achieved, their singing almost ceases. The European blackbird, for example, sings most in April and May. After July, when the main business of nesting is finished, it produces only call notes.

Scarlet macaw

13

How do parrots talk?

The shape of the parrot's beak and tongue means that it can make sounds much like human speech. Exactly why parrots can speak is still not understood, but possibly their ability may be linked with the fact that almost all are highly social, forest-living birds which keep in contact with other members of their species by frequent calls.

A young parrot kept on its own in captivity learns the sounds it hears around it and quickly realizes that repeating these sounds brings attention and companionship. These are perhaps a substitute for its normal social life. Good mimics in captivity, parrots do not imitate other sounds in the wild. Many other species such as starlings and lyre birds do mimic the sounds they hear in their everyday life.

There are more than 300 species of parrots, with a bewildering variety of brilliant hues.

Rainbow lorikeet

Dusky-orange lory

Black-capped lory

Blue-crowned hanging parrot

Do fish drink?

Anybody who has watched a fish in a tank knows that it seems to be drinking constantly. But most of the time the water taken in is not swallowed. Instead it is pushed by movements of the floor of the throat over a series of gills and expelled through slits which lie on the side of the body, just behind the head. A fish's gills are its lungs and, in fact, when it appears to be drinking, it is usually breathing.

Like any other animal a fish must "breathe" oxygen in order to live, but it obtains this oxygen from water, not air. Fish gills are made up of large numbers of delicate plates, or lamellae, so closely packed that their combined area is great. The gills are covered by a protective flap, the operculum, so they have one combined exit to the outside.

Blood flows through the lamellae in a network of blood vessels which run close to their surface. Molecules of oxygen dissolved in the water passing over the gills can therefore easily pass into the blood. The oxygenated blood then travels to all parts of the body.

Human beings use about one quarter of the available oxygen from the air that they breathe. A fish, however, removes up to four-fifths of the oxygen in the water that passes over its gills. This is possible because the blood and water flow in opposite directions through the gills. The water containing most oxygen first comes into contact with blood that requires it most urgently. As the water, with part of its oxygen removed, passes on through the mesh of gill lamellae the demands made on it are less because it is meeting blood that still carries some oxygen. As the water is finally pushed out through the gill slits, it carries little oxygen.

Fish do also need to drink water, however. When a fish drinks, it swallows the water just as we do, instead of closing off its throat to force the water through the gills. The water is filtered by the fish's kidneys and waste products and excess salts are rejected.

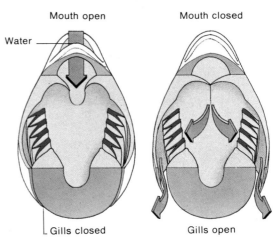

Mouth open — Water — Gills closed

Mouth closed — Gills open

When a fish's mouth is open to take in water, its gill slits are closed.

As the gills open to let the water pass out the fish shuts its mouth.

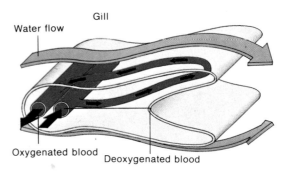

Gill

Water flow

Oxygenated blood   Deoxygenated blood

The fish's mouth and throat muscles pump a constant flow of water over the gills. Because the water and blood flow in opposite directions, the oxygen is used in the most efficient way.

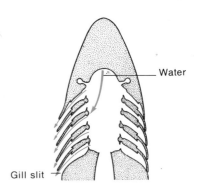

Water

Gill slit

Unlike bony fish (salmon, mackerel and so on) sharks do not have a cover protecting their gills. Each gill has its own exit to the water although all the exits open and close in unison.

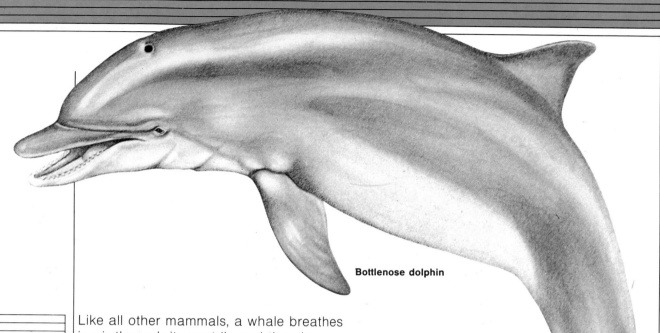

Bottlenose dolphin

15

How do whales breathe?

Like all other mammals, a whale breathes in air through its nostrils and the air passes into its lungs. Unlike other mammals, its nostrils, called a blowhole, are on the top of its head. As a whale dives, the blowhole is tightly closed against water pressure and remains shut all the time the whale is submerged. When the whale finally surfaces and breathes out, the moisture in its warm breath condenses in the cooler air to make a cloud of water vapor, just as our breath does on a cold day.

Contrary to the impression given in many old drawings of whales, they do not spout water from their blowholes. If a whale had water in its lungs it would drown, just like any other mammal.

Dolphins often "cartwheel" through the sea, opening their blowholes to take a breath just as their heads break the surface.

16

How deep do whales dive?

A sperm whale was found entangled with a submarine cable at a depth of about half a mile (0.8 km), and other species may dive as deep. Sperm whales rarely dive for less than 30 minutes and may stay under 90 minutes or more. Dolphins seldom go below 500 ft (152 m).

As a rule the filter-feeding whales (see p 84) find their food near the surface of the sea and rarely remain submerged for more than 15 minutes.

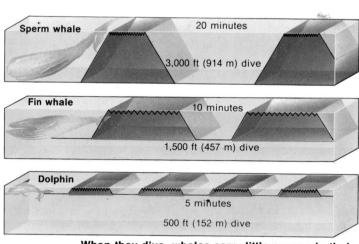

Sperm whale — 20 minutes — 3,000 ft (914 m) dive

Fin whale — 10 minutes — 1,500 ft (457 m) dive

Dolphin — 5 minutes — 500 ft (152 m) dive

When they dive, whales carry little oxygen in their lungs, but large amounts in their blood, muscles and other body tissues. The deeper they dive the longer they must spend breathing at the surface between dives.

Which animal is the fastest runner?

Of all animals the fastest runner is the cheetah, which has been timed as covering a distance of 700 yds (640 m) in 40 seconds—equivalent to a speed of 71.6 mph (115 km/h).

Many such animal speed records are calculated from speeds timed over short distances. This is because animals do not run "to order." Cheetahs, for example, do not normally run as far as a mile and usually start their high-speed attacks on prey at a distance of less than 300 ft (90 m). The cheetah can reach its maximum speed in 3 seconds but, like a human sprinter, cannot maintain this effort for long.

Plant-eating animals cannot run as fast as the cheetah, but they can keep up a reasonable speed for long periods. The fastest is probably the North American pronghorn antelope which has been timed alongside a car traveling at 35 mph (56 km/h) and did not appear tired after $3\frac{3}{4}$ miles (6 km). Over a short distance the pronghorn has been clocked at 60 mph (96.5 km/h).

Cheetah

Long powerful legs help the cheetah to run fast, but it is also assisted by the great flexibility of its back which acts like a spring to propel it on its way. The diagrams above show the sequence of leg and body movements of a cheetah running flat out.

What speeds can other animals reach in the air, on land and in water?

Following winds help animals move fast in the air. The peregrine falcon diving steeply on its prey is said to reach 224 mph (360 km/h) but in level flight it could not exceed 62 mph (100 km/h). The spinetail swift is believed to fly at about 70 mph (113 km/h) normally and to reach 105 mph (170 km/h) in display and courtship flights.

Bats fly more slowly—between 12.5 and 40 mph (20 and 65 km/h), depending on the size of species. While it is exceedingly difficult to time insects, a large dragonfly can probably reach 35 mph (57 km/h) in still air, but with a following wind flies at greater speed.

On land the lion, like the cheetah, can attain short bursts of speed. It can sprint at up to 40 mph (65 km/h) to seize its prey. Reptiles are well behind. The fastest lizard on record is the six-lined race-runner, timed for a minute at 18 mph (29 km/h), while the fastest snake can only manage 7 mph (11 km/h).

Because water is 800 times more dense than air, it is difficult for animals to swim at high speeds. All the fast-swimming fish have streamlined bodies to cut through the water with minimum resistance. The sailfish reaches speeds of 68 mph (109 km/h), while the tuna is able to move at 65 mph (105 km/h). The gentoo penguin's speed of 22 mph (36 km/h) seems modest by comparison.

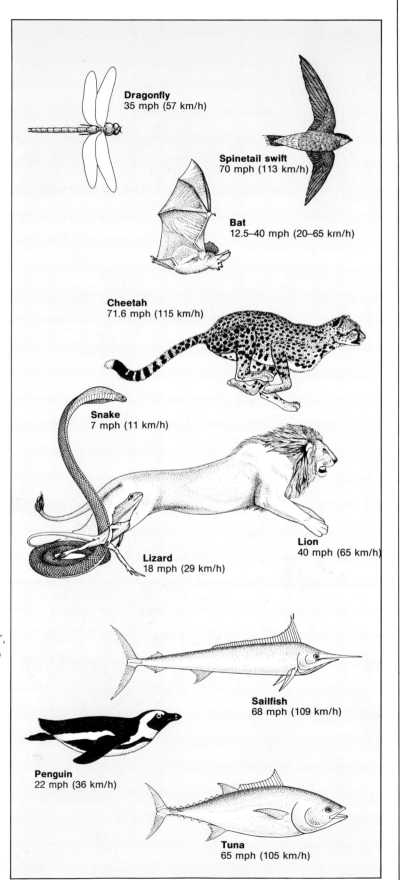

Dragonfly 35 mph (57 km/h)

Spinetail swift 70 mph (113 km/h)

Bat 12.5–40 mph (20–65 km/h)

Cheetah 71.6 mph (115 km/h)

Snake 7 mph (11 km/h)

Lion 40 mph (65 km/h)

Lizard 18 mph (29 km/h)

Sailfish 68 mph (109 km/h)

Penguin 22 mph (36 km/h)

Tuna 65 mph (105 km/h)

19

Do animals see in black and white?

Animals that are awake and active in the daytime probably see the world in color. But nocturnal animals, and those which burrow or live in the darkness of caves or the deep sea, almost certainly have no sense of color.

No all color vision is the same as ours, of course. Some insects, for example, cannot see pure red—red objects look black to them. They can, however, see ultra-violet, which is invisible to us. It used to be thought that most mammals, other than humans, monkeys and apes and perhaps squirrels, saw things in shades of gray. Now scientists believe they may see muted forms of color.

Color vision has important uses. Animals that can see colors are often brightly colored themselves and may flash colorful feathers or areas of their bodies in a form of sign language to others of their kind.

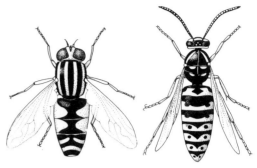

Hoverfly   **Wasp**

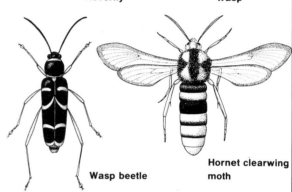

Wasp beetle   **Hornet clearwing moth**

Wasps sting to protect themselves from their enemies. Animals that have been stung are more likely to remember the experience and take action to avoid it in future if the attacker was brightly colored—as the wasp is. Various harmless insects, including hoverflies and some beetles and moths, have a similar warning coloration to wasps. Hunters avoid these mimics, despite the fact they cannot actually sting, because they look like wasps.

Stickleback

Most shallow-water fish can see color. In the breeding season male sticklebacks change color, developing red patches on their normally silvery undersides. The red coloration acts as a warning to rival sticklebacks should they trespass on another's territory. At this time male sticklebacks react violently to anything red which to them means a rival.

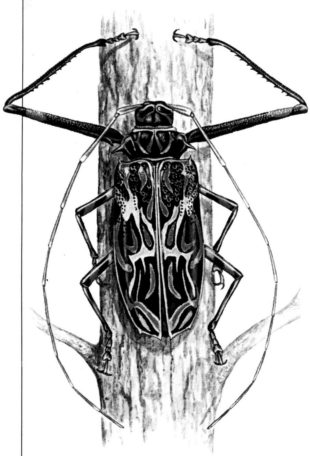

Harlequin beetle

The harlequin beetle's bright colors can probably not be seen by others of its own kind but may provide a form of camouflage. The pattern blends with that of the growths on the trunks of trees in its forest home.

Ralph Brooke's birdwing

Distasteful heliconid mimic

Harmless heliconid mimic

Birdwing butterflies are among the largest and most gorgeously colored of all insects. Like all butterflies, they can see color, and can detect color patterns that we cannot see on each other and on plants.

The black, orange and yellow coloration of many heliconid butterflies signals the fact that they taste horrible. Having tried one, hunters learn to leave them alone— thus both the butterfly's color and the hunter's color vision have a purpose.

Like many nasty tasting creatures, these butterflies are surprisingly tough and difficult to kill. A bird may peck at one, but drop it on discovering how unwholesome

it is, and the butterfly will probably survive. Other kinds of butterflies resemble the heliconids in color and fly alongside them, and these gain from their companions' reputation. Some are themselves distasteful, while others are harmless.

All brightly colored butterflies are extremely obvious to predators. Some have dull colors on the undersides of their wings to make them less visible.

How and why do some animals change coloration?

Animals usually change their color to match their backgrounds and avoid being seen by enemies—or their own prey. The chameleon is probably the most famous of natural quick change artists—it can alter its color totally in under two minutes. Even faster color changes are made by cephalopods—octopuses, squids and cuttlefish—which make a complete change in less than a second. These creatures may change color when afraid, angry or when courting as well as to merge with their surroundings. Flatfish, such as plaice, can also alter their color, but may take a couple of hours to do so.

All of these animals have a number of color cells, or chromatophores, in their skin. Each cell contains a particular pigment—black, yellow or brown, for example. The nerves controlling the cell can cause the color pigment to be spread out, so that it shows, or to be concentrated in a tiny area, so it is not seen on the surface.

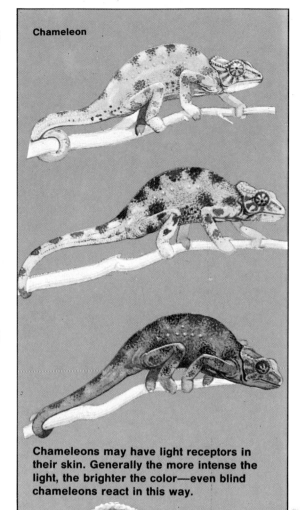

Chameleon

Chameleons may have light receptors in their skin. Generally the more intense the light, the brighter the color—even blind chameleons react in this way.

Chameleons do not change color consciously, but they usually match their backgrounds well. This keeps them hidden from their enemies and allows them to creep up unnoticed on their own prey. A chameleon's color also changes with its mood. An angry chameleon darkens in color; one that is afraid turns almost white.

Chameleon

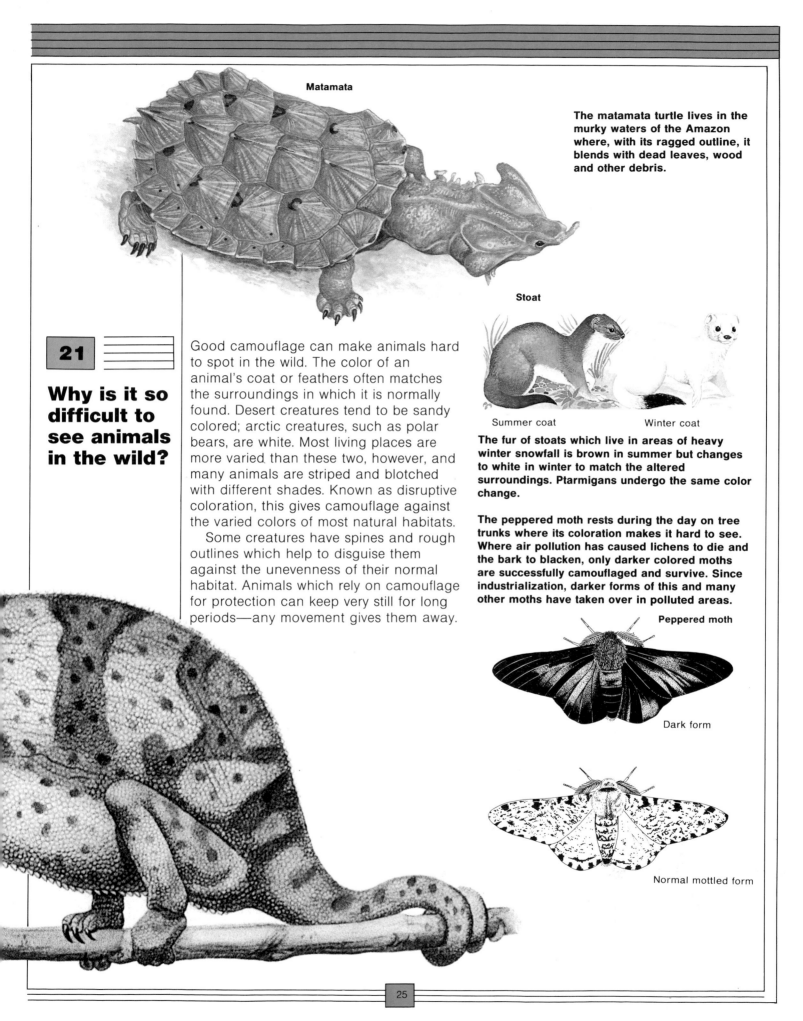

Matamata

The matamata turtle lives in the murky waters of the Amazon where, with its ragged outline, it blends with dead leaves, wood and other debris.

Stoat

Summer coat   Winter coat

The fur of stoats which live in areas of heavy winter snowfall is brown in summer but changes to white in winter to match the altered surroundings. Ptarmigans undergo the same color change.

The peppered moth rests during the day on tree trunks where its coloration makes it hard to see. Where air pollution has caused lichens to die and the bark to blacken, only darker colored moths are successfully camouflaged and survive. Since industrialization, darker forms of this and many other moths have taken over in polluted areas.

Peppered moth

Dark form

Normal mottled form

21

Why is it so difficult to see animals in the wild?

Good camouflage can make animals hard to spot in the wild. The color of an animal's coat or feathers often matches the surroundings in which it is normally found. Desert creatures tend to be sandy colored; arctic creatures, such as polar bears, are white. Most living places are more varied than these two, however, and many animals are striped and blotched with different shades. Known as disruptive coloration, this gives camouflage against the varied colors of most natural habitats.

Some creatures have spines and rough outlines which help to disguise them against the unevenness of their normal habitat. Animals which rely on camouflage for protection can keep very still for long periods—any movement gives them away.

22

Why do tigers have stripes?

The stripes which make a tiger so obvious in the zoo help it merge perfectly with its surroundings in its natural home of forest and scrubland. As well as blending with the lines of tall grasses in which the tiger hides, the stripes break up the body outline and make it harder to see. Such camouflage is vital for the tiger's hunting success. Only because it is so hard to see can the tiger approach within striking distance of its quarry.

The zebra is the only other large animal with strong vertical stripes. It has been suggested that the zebra's stripes, too, are for camouflage but this is not so; in their open country home zebras are very obvious. Recent studies have shown that zebras are extremely social animals and that their stripes, which are different in every individual, are a means of recognizing members of their own family group and their neighbors.

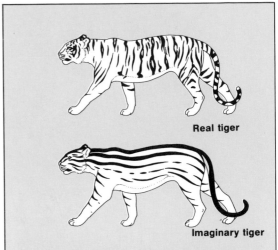

Real tiger

Imaginary tiger

Some forest animals, such as okapi and young wild pigs and tapirs, are camouflaged by horizontal lines on their bodies. On a tiger such a pattern would not work. While vertical stripes merge with the lines of the tall grasses among which the tiger hides, horizontal stripes would cut across them, making the animal more obvious.

By approaching its quarry from downwind, remaining well hidden and moving silently on its padded feet, the tiger can hope to get near enough to make a final, fatal pounce. The tiger may weigh 500 lb (226 kg) or more and a blow from one of its powerful paws breaks the neck of most victims.

Tiger

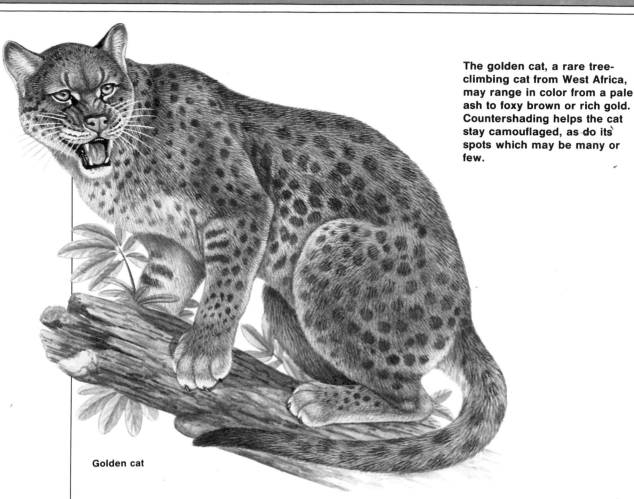

The golden cat, a rare tree-climbing cat from West Africa, may range in color from a pale ash to foxy brown or rich gold. Countershading helps the cat stay camouflaged, as do its spots which may be many or few.

Golden cat

23

Why are animals usually paler on their stomachs than on their backs?

Almost all animals are countershaded, that is, more intensely colored on their backs than on their undersides. Since light generally falls on a creature from above, the lower half of its body will tend to be in the shadow of its upper parts and appear darker. These shadows can make an animal which is the same color all over look rounder and more obvious. But if the undersides are paler, this effect is lessened and the creature appears flatter and is more difficult to see.

Many large creatures, including some whales and sharks, are countershaded. A few fish have stomachs darker than their backs—reverse countershading—but they swim upsidedown so the effect is the same. Some caterpillars are also reversely countershaded and hang upsidedown from their food plants. In one experiment dead caterpillars were fixed to the upper side of twigs—lighter side uppermost. Birds soon spotted and ate them, but did not notice the countershaded, live insects clinging below the branches.

Palm civet

Servaline genet

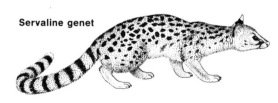

Linsang

The spotted and striped coats of some small forest-living predators successfully camouflage their owners. The markings break up the outline of the body and merge with the dappled forest light to deceive the eye. Countershading makes their outline even more shadowy and hard to see, since their markings seem to disappear into nowhere.

Sword-billed hummingbird

Frilled coquette

White-tipped sicklebill

Marvelous spatuletail

The smallest hummingbirds weigh only 0.07 oz (2 g), less than many insects. The birds' bills vary greatly in shape, each specialized to probe particular sorts of flowers for nectar and tiny insects.

24

Do humming-birds hum?

Hummingbirds do hum, but the low-pitched buzzing sound is made by their wings, not their voices. When they fly, hummingbirds beat their wings constantly and very fast—in some species more than 50 times a second. These continuous wing movements make an uninterrupted hum which gives the birds their name.

The flight of hummingbirds is much more energetic than that of other birds. The ratio between the area of their wings and the weight of their body is similar to that of most other birds but their flying muscles are relatively huge. These muscles provide the energy for them to

beat their wings so fast that they can hover and fly backward as well as fly normally.

The ability to hover is crucial to the hummingbird. It feeds largely on nectar from flowers and, since there is rarely a convenient perch in front of the flower, the bird needs to hold itself in midair while it feeds—something it can only do by the exhausting process of hovering. When a hummingbird hovers, its body is held vertically and its wings moved backward and forward, not up and down as in normal flight. This movement gives power on both wingbeats.

How did birds of paradise get their name?

Blue bird of paradise

In the fifteenth century, Europeans first began to explore and trade with the East. Among items brought back from New Guinea were bird skins, with full plumage but usually with the feet and legs cut off by the native hunters. Some of these birds were so beautiful that people called them birds of paradise. They thought them too exquisite to be earthly birds and imagined them constantly airborne in paradise with no need of feet for perching.

Male birds of paradise are brilliantly colored, often with long, filmy or iridescent plumes. To attract their drab-colored mates, male birds may even hang upsidedown to show off their feathers.

Do animals show their age?

Although it is harder to guess at the age of an animal than a human, there are some revealing signs. In male deer, for instance, the antlers give a clue to age. These increase in size and complexity until, in old age, they begin to shrink. Similarly, the horn size in animals such as sheep increases with age. Badly worn teeth can be a sign of old age.

A few mammals, including the whales and elephants, grow rapidly in their early years and slowly continue to increase in size for the rest of their lives. Some crocodiles and fish have similar patterns of growth. All these animals show their age by their size: if they are big for the size range of their species, they are probably old. Many birds grow so quickly that they are as big as their parents when they leave the nest, but in many species juvenile birds are identified by their different colored plumage.

Some creatures grow in spurts at certain times of year. Their age shows in growth rings. These rings are seen, for example, on the scales of fish and some reptiles, on the horny ear plugs of baleen whales and the teeth of sperm whales.

Some creatures have very short lifespans. Mice and shrews, for example,

A baby orang-utan has a rounded head and face and may look startlingly human. It keeps this look through its juvenile years.

A young adult orang has a moderately rounded face and is starting to develop fatty areas under the chin.

A fully adult male orang has large flaps of fatty tissue surrounding the face. These, like a deer's antlers, seem to increase the animal's social status and show it to be adult.

rarely survive more than a year. Some insects have a long larval period but their active, adult life is measured in weeks or even days. A butterfly with tattered wings has probably been flying for several weeks and does not have much longer to live.

How long do animals live?

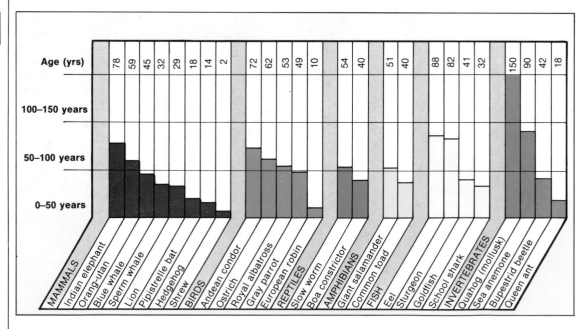

Age (yrs)																									
MAMMALS	78	59	45	32	29	18	14	2																	
BIRDS									72	62	53	49	10												
REPTILES														54	40										
AMPHIBIANS																51	40								
FISH																		88	82	41	32				
INVERTEBRATES																						150	90	42	18

MAMMALS: Indian elephant, Orang-utan, Blue whale, Sperm whale, Lion, Pipistrelle bat, Hedgehog, Shrew; BIRDS: Andean condor, Ostrich, Royal albatross, Gray parrot, European robin; REPTILES: Slow worm, Boa constrictor; AMPHIBIANS: Giant salamander, Common toad; FISH: Eel, Sturgeon, Goldfish, School shark; INVERTEBRATES: Quahog (mollusk), Sea anemone, Bupestrid beetle, Queen ant

The ages shown here were mostly recorded in captivity. Clearly, animals living in safety with plenty of food will tend to live longer than animals in the wild which are at the mercy of predators and other hazards.

Behavior changes with age, and can be a clue to an animal's stage of development. In their early days, young primates cling to their mothers. As they become more independent they are playful and adventurous; only when they are adults is their behavior at its most complex. Old animals suffering from degenerative diseases, such as arthritis, may be forced to slow down.

Orang-utan

Which are the biggest and the smallest animals?

Animals vary in size from protozoans, creatures so tiny that several hundred could cluster on one comma on this page, to the blue whale which, at over 100 ft (30 m) long, is the largest creature ever to have lived. Other sea-dwelling giants include huge jellyfish, which trail tentacles 120 ft (36.5 m) long, and giant squid. The largest fish is the whale shark.

The African elephant is the heaviest land animal and weighs about 11,570 lb (5,248 kg). Like all large land creatures it is a plant eater. Even the bears, which are the bulkiest carnivores, eke out their diet with plant foods. The largest bird, the ostrich, is about 97,000 times the bulk of the smallest, but the wandering albatross has the largest wingspan. Even the insect world has its giants. Stick insects are the longest, while goliath beetles at 2 to 3 oz (56–85 g) are the bulkiest.

Small mammals include several species of shrew which measure between 1½ and 2 in (3.5–5 cm) plus another inch of tail, and the hog-nosed bat which weighs no more than 0.07 oz (2 g). The smallest bird, the bee hummingbird of Cuba, weighs about the same or slightly less than the hog-nosed bat, while the smallest fish, the pygmy dwarf goby, is still tinier.

Bears are the bulkiest carnivores. Although they do eat some flesh, about 70 percent of their diet is plant food.

What are the advantages of being very big or very small?

Both extremes of size have their advantages—and their disadvantages. Big creatures are less likely to be attacked by predators and, if they are, are better able to resist. However, they need to find vast amounts of food to fuel their large bodies. Small creatures take little from their surroundings, so many individuals can occupy the same space as one large creature. They can hide from enemies but, if caught, are easily killed.

Small creatures are more at the mercy of weather changes than are large ones, but, because they are faster breeders, they can more quickly build up numbers again.

The figures given here are averages rather than extremes. Male or female is specified where the sexes differ.

African elephant (male)
Weight: 11,570 lb (5,248 kg)
Shoulder height: 10.5 ft (3.2 m)

Kodiak bear (male)
Weight: 1,175 lb (533 kg)
Length: 8 ft (2.4 m)

Blue whale (female)
Length: 100 ft (30.4 m)
Estimated weight: 100 tons (98.4 tonnes)

Estuarine crocodile
Length: up to 20 ft (6 m)
Weight: 2,418 lb (1,097 kg)

Whale shark
Length: 28 ft (1.58 m) or more
Estimated weight: 19 tons (19.3 tonnes)

Ostrich (male)
Height: 8 ft (2.4 m)
Weight: 270 lb (122 kg)

Reticulated python
Length: up to 32 ft 9 in (10 m)
Weight: 320 lb (145 kg)

Human
Height: up to 7 ft (2.1 m)
Weight: average 180 lb (81.6 kg)

Wandering albatross (male)
Wingspan: 10 ft (3 m)
Weight: 28 lb (12.7 kg)

Hog-nosed bat
Length: 1.5 in (3.8 cm)
Weight: 0.07 oz (2 g)

Bee hummingbird
Length: 2 in (5 cm)
Weight: 0.07 oz (2 g)

Pygmy dwarf goby
Length: 0.3 in (0.8 cm)
Weight: 0.0017 oz (5 mg)

Stick insect
Length: up to 20 in (51 cm)

Why are birds' beaks so many different shapes?

A bird has a beak of the shape best suited to its lifestyle—and in particular, to what it eats, and how. Beaks come in many different shapes because birds eat a wide range of foods and beak shape gives a clue to a bird's diet. Insect eaters, for example, have thin pointed bills for picking up their food; eagles and hawks have strong hooked beaks for tearing apart the flesh of their prey.

A bird cannot use its wings for holding objects so the beak has to be suitably shaped to double as the bird's hands for holding food and nesting material.

Whatever its shape and size, a bird's beak is also used for preening—keeping the plumage clean. With it, the bird can remove any dirt, parasites or loose feathers from its body.

Garden warbler

The garden warbler has a finely pointed beak, the shape best suited to its habit of picking aphids and other small insects off the leaves and bushes. It may also take the tiny eggs and larvae of insects.

Birds of prey have strong hooked beaks, suitable for tearing flesh apart as they feed. One bird of prey, the Everglade kite, which feeds on snails, has a particularly long and pointed upper bill. Using this, it can pull the snail's flesh out of the shell.

Everglade kite

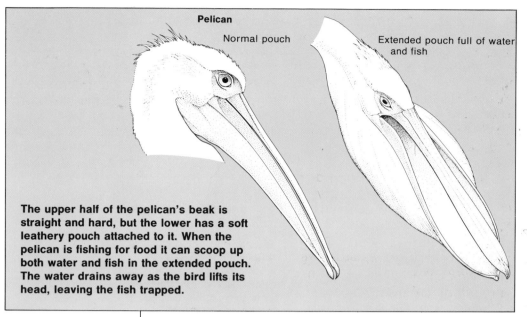

Pelican

Normal pouch

Extended pouch full of water and fish

The upper half of the pelican's beak is straight and hard, but the lower has a soft leathery pouch attached to it. When the pelican is fishing for food it can scoop up both water and fish in the extended pouch. The water drains away as the bird lifts its head, leaving the fish trapped.

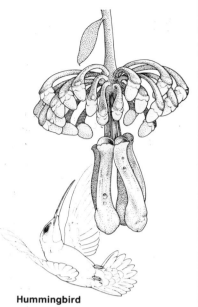

Hummingbird

Hummingbirds have long slender pointed bills which house brush-tipped tongues. With such beaks, the birds can reach into long-tubed blossoms to sip the nectar.

Toucan

Toucans have larger beaks, compared with their body size, than any other birds. With these, they can reach berries and fruit growing on twigs too slender for them to perch on. Toucans can then neatly toss their food back into their throats.

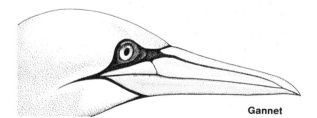

Gannet

Like most fish-eating diving birds the gannet has a long pointed bill, ideally shaped for holding slippery fish. The gannet dives near its prey, snatching it while returning to the surface.

Finch

The finch's short, conical beak is specially adapted for feeding on seeds. The bird picks up a seed which wedges into a groove inside the beak. As the beak closes, the seed husk is split. The bird then peels off the husk with its tongue, discards it and swallows the seed. Different kinds of finch eat seeds of varying hardness and size. The hawfinch can even crack olive pits for their kernels.

Garganey duck

The flattened bill of the garganey, like that of many ducks, has a fringe of small plates on the inside. These retain the insects and plants the duck gathers from the water.

31

Why does a snake have a forked tongue?

The snake's forked tongue helps it track down prey. As the snake hunts for a meal, it is constantly flicking out its tongue. Each time the tongue returns to the snake's mouth it brings with it clues from the immediate environment to a hollow in the roof of the mouth. Known as Jacobson's organ, this hollow is lined with sensitive cells which enable the snake to "taste" the track of its prey. Because the tongue is forked it covers a wide area, so the snake can find its prey more easily.

32

How do rattlesnakes rattle?

At the end of the rattlesnake's body are separate segments of horny material which the snake can vibrate rapidly, creating a loud buzzing noise. Known as the rattle, these segments are formed by scales from the tip of the tail that are left behind when the snake sheds its skin (molts). With each molt, the rattle grows, but the segments are fragile and break easily, usually after no more than six to eight have been formed.

The noise made by the vibrating rattle, which is like the sound of a burst of steam, is used by the rattlesnake when alarmed. It is used to warn off enemies.

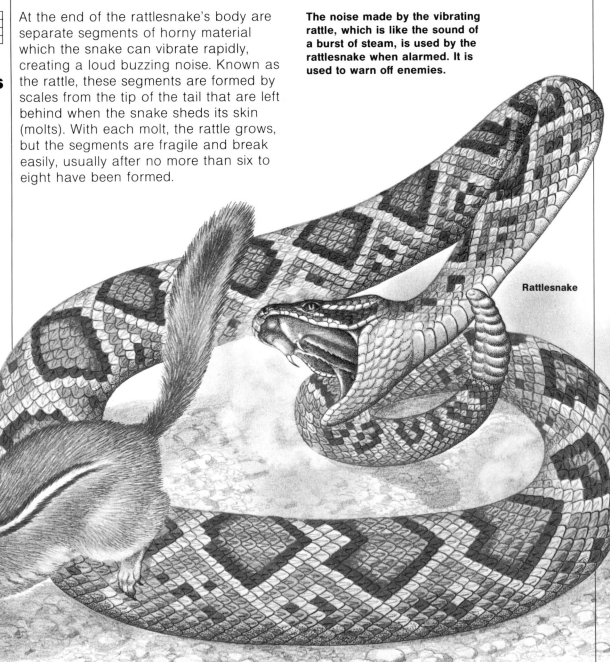

Rattlesnake

33

Why don't snakes have legs?

The ancestors of snakes were animals with legs and even today some kinds of snakes, such as many pythons and boas, have tiny, spurlike hind legs. These are useless for moving, but are sometimes used by males and females in pre-mating displays.

Today's snakes are thought to have evolved from burrowing, lizardlike creatures. Some lizards still spend most of their lives underground and move by sideways snakelike movements of their bodies, as though they were swimming through the soil or sand. Lizards like these have tiny legs or none at all.

Most snakes live on the surface of the ground. Some live in burrows, others have taken to life in the trees and yet others live in the sea. However, none can regrow the legs which have been lost in the course of evolution. They must use the sideways "swimming" movements of the burrowing lizards, pegging their position against stones or vegetation to get some leverage.

Paradise tree snake

34

How do snakes move?

A snake normally moves by throwing its body into a series of curves and then pushing itself along from these curves. Ripples of movement pass from the head down to the tail as a selection of muscles on one side of the body tighten and those on the opposite side relax.

Thick-bodied snakes, such as pythons, can move forward almost in a straight line, helped by the grip given by large scales on the animal's underside. The scales are free on the back edges and catch and hold against any roughness beneath them, allowing the snake to pull itself forward.

An impression of speed is given by the sideways movements of snakes but they rarely move at more than 4 mph (6.5 km/h). The record for a snake timed over a measured distance is held by a mamba which traveled for 140 ft (43 m) at 7 mph (11 km/h).

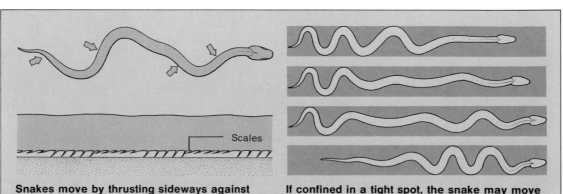

Scales

Snakes move by thrusting sideways against objects on the ground, or by hauling themselves forward with the help of scales on the belly.

If confined in a tight spot, the snake may move concertina-style, pressing itself against obstacles, then straightening out to move forward.

35

Why do animals sleep?

Although sleep takes up a large proportion of the lives of most animals with backbones—including humans—nobody is certain of its real purpose. One suggestion is that once a creature has enough food, shelter and other necessities, sleep keeps it out of trouble and saves it wasting any further energy.

Like humans, animals normally suffer if they are deprived of sleep although some birds, such as those that live in the continuous daylight of the Arctic summer, sleep little during that season with no apparent ill effects. Many mammals spend a large part of their day asleep: opossums sleep for about 19 hours a day. Lions spend as much as 20 hours a day napping and resting.

The times at which animals sleep and wake vary. Some are awake and alert in the daytime—these are diurnal animals; others are nocturnal—they are awake at night. Like shift-workers, the two types can make use of the same resources. For example, owls can hunt at night in an area taken over by hawks in the day.

Animals are active at night for a variety of reasons. Owls and other hunters avoid competition with daytime predators. Mice can use the same food sources as daytime plant and seed eaters, while frogs and other amphibians prefer the moist night air to the dry daytime atmosphere.

36

Do animals dream?

When a sleeping dog twitches and whimpers it is easy to imagine that it is dreaming of chasing rabbits or the neighbor's cat. But at that moment it is certainly not dreaming—the brain switches off such body movements while a dream is going on. Just before this active phase the dog may well have been dreaming, however. Dogs, cats and other mammals are like humans in so many ways, it is quite possible that they dream.

Scientific studies show that sleep is more than a period of restful blackout—sleeping or waking, brain activity is continuous and varied. Nerve cells at the surface send out regular impulses. A machine which measures these shows that as an animal falls asleep the waves become larger, but less frequent.

After a period which varies with the species (90 minutes in humans, 25 in cats) there is an abrupt change in brain waves. The brain is highly aroused and the eyes, although closed, make rapid scanning movements, usually from side to side. This Rapid Eye Movement (REM) sleep is associated with dreaming in humans. Since all mammals experience REM, it is likely that they, too, dream.

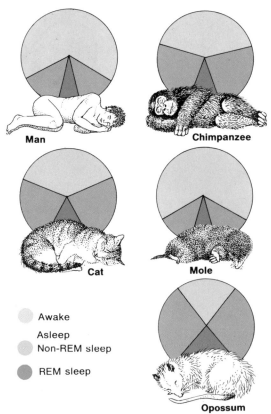

Awake

Asleep
Non-REM sleep

REM sleep

All mammals have periods of REM sleep and non-REM sleep. In hunters, such as humans and dogs, 20 to 30 percent of their sleep is REM; in plant-eaters, such as sheep, only about 3 percent is REM. Birds and reptiles have little REM sleep and REM has been observed only once in a fish.

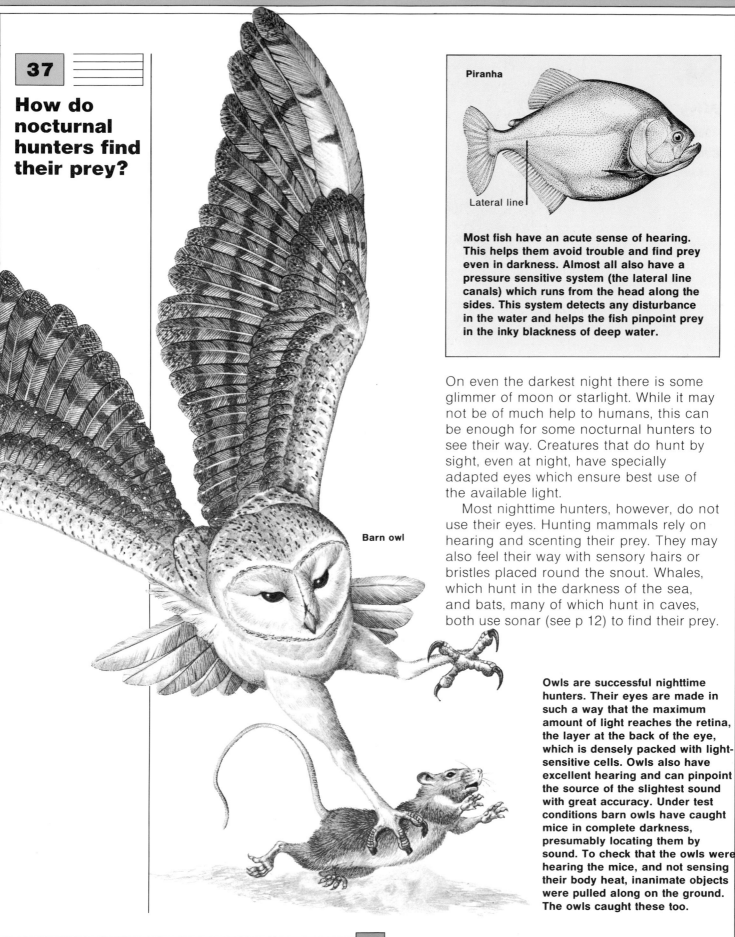

How do nocturnal hunters find their prey?

Piranha

Lateral line

Most fish have an acute sense of hearing. This helps them avoid trouble and find prey even in darkness. Almost all also have a pressure sensitive system (the lateral line canals) which runs from the head along the sides. This system detects any disturbance in the water and helps the fish pinpoint prey in the inky blackness of deep water.

On even the darkest night there is some glimmer of moon or starlight. While it may not be of much help to humans, this can be enough for some nocturnal hunters to see their way. Creatures that do hunt by sight, even at night, have specially adapted eyes which ensure best use of the available light.

Most nighttime hunters, however, do not use their eyes. Hunting mammals rely on hearing and scenting their prey. They may also feel their way with sensory hairs or bristles placed round the snout. Whales, which hunt in the darkness of the sea, and bats, many of which hunt in caves, both use sonar (see p 12) to find their prey.

Barn owl

Owls are successful nighttime hunters. Their eyes are made in such a way that the maximum amount of light reaches the retina, the layer at the back of the eye, which is densely packed with light-sensitive cells. Owls also have excellent hearing and can pinpoint the source of the slightest sound with great accuracy. Under test conditions barn owls have caught mice in complete darkness, presumably locating them by sound. To check that the owls were hearing the mice, and not sensing their body heat, inanimate objects were pulled along on the ground. The owls caught these too.

38

Why do some animals hibernate?

In some parts of the world winter weather cuts off food supplies and makes it hard for animals to survive. In these areas some creatures solve the problem by dropping into a deep torpor, or hibernation, through the winter. During this period, the animal's body uses as little energy as possible; it does not replace that energy by eating, so its body fat supplies must provide it. The temperature of a hibernating animal falls until it is close to that of the surrounding air, and even its breathing and heartbeat rate are slower than normal. As a result of all these measures the hibernating animal can survive, using about one-fiftieth or less of its usual energy.

Animals that hibernate are all fairly small; the largest are marmots, which weigh about 15 lb (6.8 kg). Bigger creatures such as badgers and bears snooze through long periods of bad weather, but their energy use is simply that of normal sleep, not the reduced levels of true hibernation.

Bats, which cannot constantly keep up the high energy output needed for flight, drop into mini-hibernation at their roosts, even in the summertime. They become torpid—their body temperature drops and they enter a sluggish, dormant state. Hummingbirds, which use a great deal of energy in their hovering flight, also become torpid at night and save precious energy for the daytime.

Golden-mantled ground squirrel

Hibernating animals sleep curled up—this reduces the surface area over which they can lose body heat. They may wake now and then, taking a couple of hours over the process. Periods of waking are especially important when the temperature falls dramatically. If the sleeping creature's body tissues were to freeze it would die, so it wakes and warms itself with a brief spell of normal energy output.

Deep sleep

Waking

Awake

39

How do animals prepare for hibernation?

Hedgehog

During summer and fall, animals that hibernate eat a great deal of food and become very fat. As the weather cools they make well-insulated hibernating dens. At the start of hibernation a hedgehog's temperature falls from its normal 95° Fahrenheit to about 50°F. Its heartbeat slows from over 100 to less than 20 beats a minute and it may breathe only once every few minutes.

40

Do animals other than mammals hibernate?

Reptiles and amphibians, insects and other animals without backbones that live in cool places hibernate regularly. Their activity levels are geared to the temperature of their surroundings and it is easy for them to sink into a drowsy state as the temperature falls.

Sea fish, apart from the great basking shark, rarely hibernate. Although several kinds of birds, such as mousebirds, swifts, sunbirds, hummingbirds and titmice, can become partially torpid, only one, the Nuttall's poorwill, really hibernates.

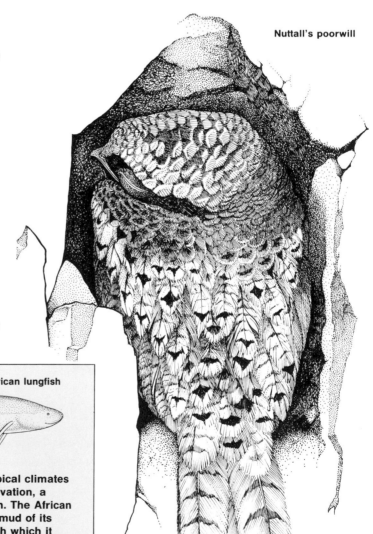

Nuttall's poorwill

African lungfish

During the dry season in hot tropical climates some animals may drop into estivation, a torpid state similar to hibernation. The African lungfish burrows into the drying mud of its home, leaving an air hole through which it breathes. Here it sleeps until the rains come again.

Why do animals migrate?

Breeding and feeding are the two main reasons for migration. Animals that migrate may do so to guarantee the right conditions for breeding (which may be different from their requirements the rest of the year) or to find food supplies in seasons of cold weather or drought. By migrating between two parts of the world animals can get the best of both: for example, spending summer in the northern hemisphere then moving south to catch summer there and avoid the northern winter.

Birds such as swallows are the most familiar migrants, but many other kinds of creatures, such as insects, fish, whales and land mammals also migrate.

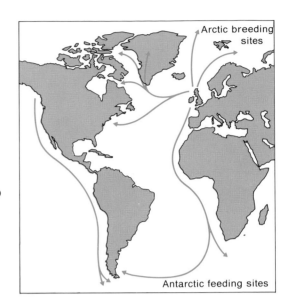

Arctic breeding sites

Antarctic feeding sites

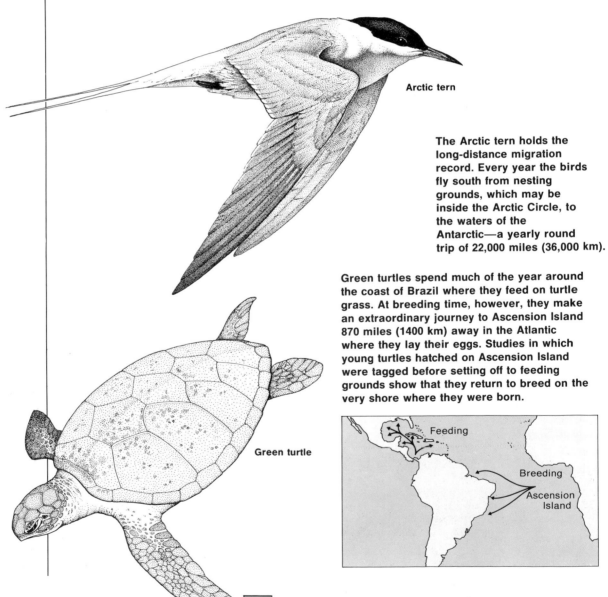

Arctic tern

The Arctic tern holds the long-distance migration record. Every year the birds fly south from nesting grounds, which may be inside the Arctic Circle, to the waters of the Antarctic—a yearly round trip of 22,000 miles (36,000 km).

Green turtles spend much of the year around the coast of Brazil where they feed on turtle grass. At breeding time, however, they make an extraordinary journey to Ascension Island 870 miles (1400 km) away in the Atlantic where they lay their eggs. Studies in which young turtles hatched on Ascension Island were tagged before setting off to feeding grounds show that they return to breed on the very shore where they were born.

Green turtle

Feeding

Breeding

Ascension Island

How do they find their way?

Animals, such as caribou or wildebeest, which migrate over land, use mountain ranges, river valleys and other such landmarks to guide them. Others use less obvious means. Green turtles, for example, seem to be guided to their own tiny breeding grounds on Ascension Island in the mid-Atlantic by a distinctive "island flavor" in the sea. The turtles detect this in the water currents and follow it from their feeding areas off the coast of Brazil.

There are migrants which use navigation methods similar to those employed by human sailors. Some marine creatures and others that migrate at night have a built-in knowledge of the stars and planets by which they navigate. Some birds and fish have crystals of magnetite in their bodies which act as natural compasses. Migrants also learn from each other. Young migrate with old and learn the routes that they should take.

Salmon migrate from the rivers where they were spawned and spent the first years of their lives to the open ocean where they mature. After two or three years they return to the waters in which they were born where they now mate and lay their eggs. Most then die, exhausted by a journey during which they do not feed.

In the past, when swallows flew south for the summer people thought they had hidden or gone to sleep somewhere. They did not realize that small creatures could travel such long distances. Nowadays migrating flocks are watched and counted by naturalists, tracked by radar and even airplanes. Creatures may also be given numbered metal tags so they can be identified when found thousands of miles from where they were originally tagged.

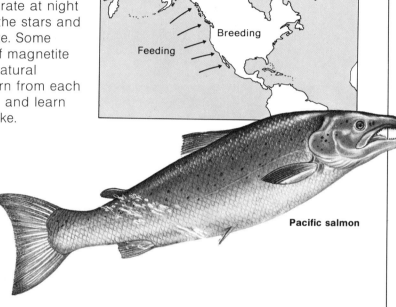

Breeding

Feeding

Pacific salmon

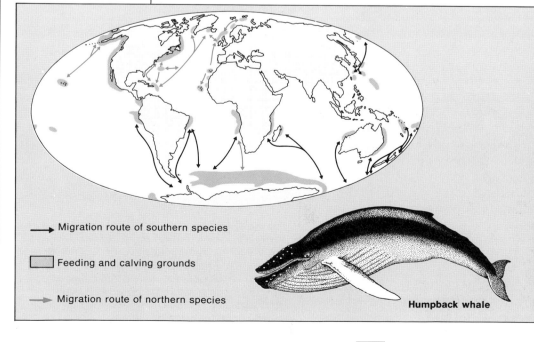

→ Migration route of southern species

▭ Feeding and calving grounds

→ Migration route of northern species

Humpback whale

There are humpback whales in the waters of both the Arctic and Antarctic. Although icy cold, these waters are rich in food supplies, including vast numbers of krill, the tiny shrimplike creatures which the whales feed on. These ideal feeding grounds would, however, be too cold for newborn young, so the whales migrate to the warmer waters of the Equator in the breeding season. Here, the calves are born and suckled until they are large and strong enough to make the return journey. Although both northern and southern populations travel toward the Equator, they both do so in their particular winters which never coincide.

43

Why do birds beat their wings to fly but airplanes don't?

Pigeon

Birds have wings like airplanes do, but they use them in a different way. Any flying object needs to have something to give it power for forward movement and something to react with the air flow to give lift—the force which holds the object above ground. An airplane has an engine

Birds use more energy when taking off than in level flight. Their wing movements are greater and the tail is spread and turned down to prevent stalling—loss of lift at low speeds.

to provide power, so that the wings are used only to give lift. The wings of a flying animal are part of the power system; beating them gives the thrust to move forward.

In birds, lift is provided by the back part of the wing, which moves little with each beat, and the tail, which comes into play mostly at slow speeds. When flying slowly, a bird can spread its wings at the tips to add to the lift over the upper surface. A small group of feathers, the alula, on the main angle of the wing can be erected for the same purpose.

Flying uses lots of energy and requires large amounts of fuel (food) and oxygen. For their size, birds eat a great deal and their breathing and digestion are very efficient. To match the energy output of a hummingbird, for example, a human would need a daily calorie intake equivalent to 370 pounds (168 kg) of potatoes.

44

Why do birds have feathers?

Feathers keep a bird's body warm and, because they make up the organs of flight—the wings and tail—enable it to fly. Each feather grows from a small follicle, or cavity, in the skin. In most birds these lie in definite patterns although an undercoat of down may cover the whole body.

Feathers are made of keratin—the same material from which human hair and fingernails are made. They contain a high proportion of air so are very light. Each feather has a hollow central quill with a series of branches or barbs growing from its sides. In most there are small side branches, barbules, on the barbs. These mesh with each other, like the teeth of a zip fastener, to make the body, or vane, of the feather.

The flight feathers of the wings and tail are large and strong, while the feathers covering the body are smaller. Even these small feathers help in the process of flight by keeping the surface of the bird's body streamlined.

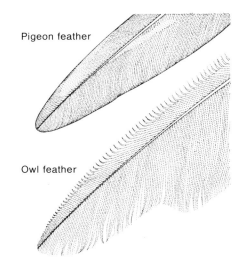

Pigeon feather

Owl feather

The leading edge of each flight feather, which must face strong air pressures, is narrower and stiffer than its trailing edge. In many birds the end of the trailing edge is narrowed so that the wing tips can be spread out in slow flight; this adjusts lift and prevents stalling. Even owls' feathers, which are soft and fluffy to muffle the normal sounds of flight, have this feature.

How fast do birds beat their wings?

The rate at which birds beat their wings varies with the way they fly. A hovering hummingbird may beat its wings more than 60 times a second. Pheasants, with their broad, highly arched wings, are very agile in flight and beat their wings almost constantly. Owls use slow wing beats and little energy.

Some of the largest flying birds beat their wings very little. Vultures and condors, for example, seek out rising currents of hot air. They ride these currents, or thermals, circling slowly for hours without once flapping their wings. Large sea birds, such as albatrosses, use wind and updrafts of air from the surface of the waves so they, too, rarely beat their wings except on take-off.

Hooded crow

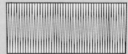

Hummingbird

Stock dove

The flight of most birds is powered by the downward strokes of the wings. This downward movement provides the thrust which makes the bird accelerate. Wing movements are driven by the bird's flight muscles which can account for about one quarter of its weight.

Eagles, gulls and other large flying birds beat their wings more slowly than small birds such as sparrows and thrushes. The large birds have a greater expanse of wing area compared to their body size.

In hovering flight, hummingbirds beat their wings more than 60 times a second.

The stock dove can fly fast for long distances, flapping its wings about 12 times a second.

The hooded crow beats its wings 6 or 8 times a second. It generally flies slowly but spreads out its tapered primary feathers to stop itself stalling.

Even in flapping flight gulls move their wings slowly, only about twice a second. They are masters at making the wind support them.

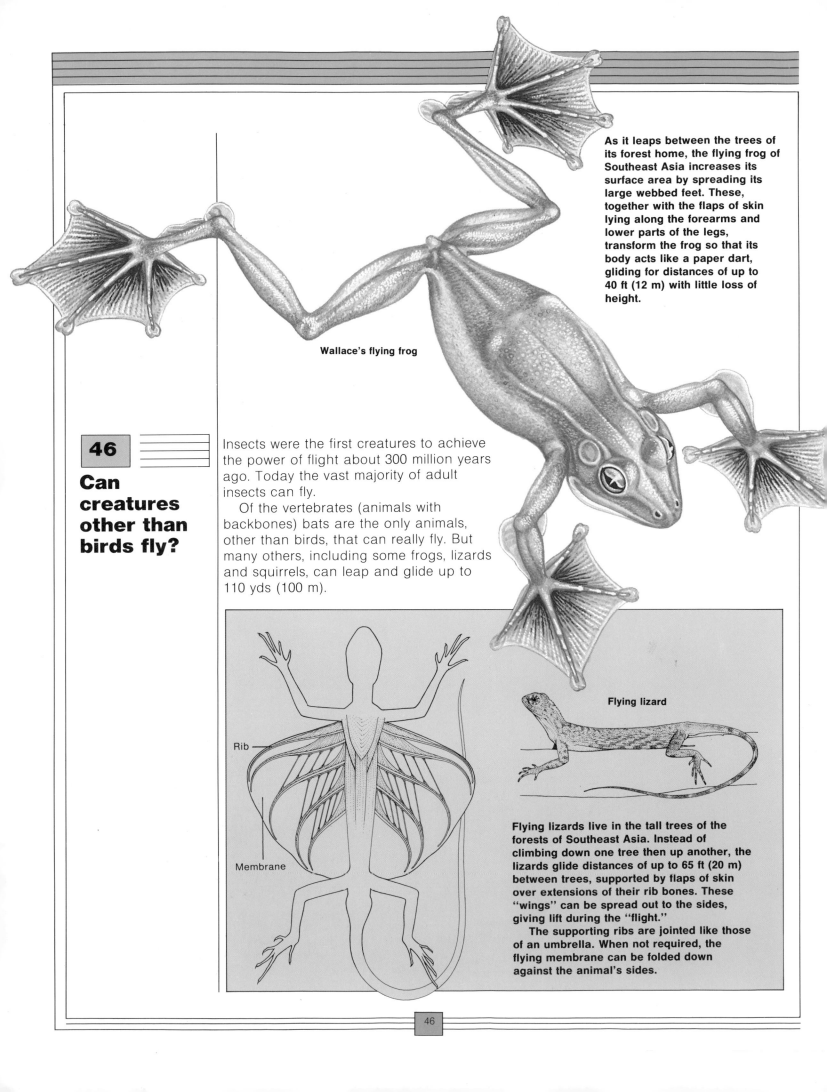

As it leaps between the trees of its forest home, the flying frog of Southeast Asia increases its surface area by spreading its large webbed feet. These, together with the flaps of skin lying along the forearms and lower parts of the legs, transform the frog so that its body acts like a paper dart, gliding for distances of up to 40 ft (12 m) with little loss of height.

Wallace's flying frog

46

Can creatures other than birds fly?

Insects were the first creatures to achieve the power of flight about 300 million years ago. Today the vast majority of adult insects can fly.

Of the vertebrates (animals with backbones) bats are the only animals, other than birds, that can really fly. But many others, including some frogs, lizards and squirrels, can leap and glide up to 110 yds (100 m).

Rib

Membrane

Flying lizard

Flying lizards live in the tall trees of the forests of Southeast Asia. Instead of climbing down one tree then up another, the lizards glide distances of up to 65 ft (20 m) between trees, supported by flaps of skin over extensions of their rib bones. These "wings" can be spread out to the sides, giving lift during the "flight."

The supporting ribs are jointed like those of an umbrella. When not required, the flying membrane can be folded down against the animal's sides.

Many squirrels increase their chances of finding food and escaping from enemies by leaping and gliding between trees. Their glides are supported by flying membranes, or patagiums—flaps of skin between the wrists and ankles. In Australasia, marsupial gliders, such as the pygmy glider of New Guinea, live a similar life to squirrels. As it leaps, the glider spreads its limbs, so extending the parachutelike flying membrane which supports it.

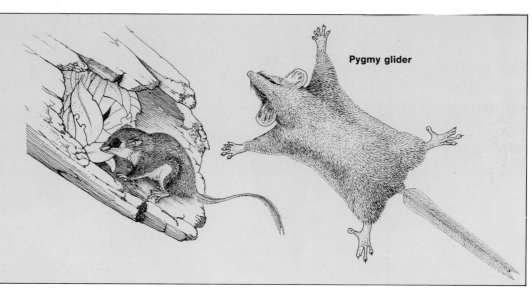

Pygmy glider

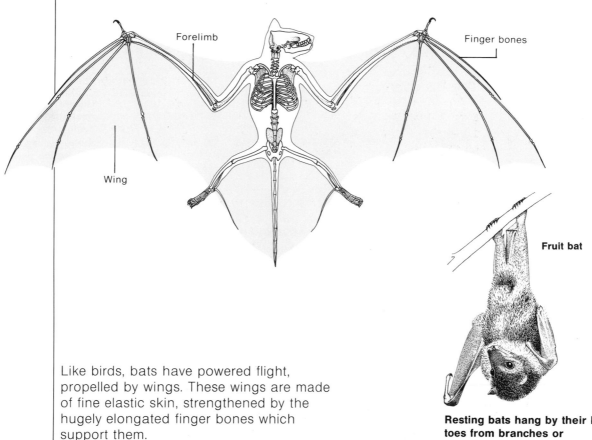

Forelimb

Finger bones

Wing

Fruit bat

Like birds, bats have powered flight, propelled by wings. These wings are made of fine elastic skin, strengthened by the hugely elongated finger bones which support them.

Bat flight seems slow and erratic compared with that of most birds, but the bat's flying muscles are more complex in their structure than bird flight muscles. The reason is that bats need to fly with great precision when pursuing their prey or maneuvering in the cramped and often extremely crowded caves in which they commonly roost.

Resting bats hang by their hind toes from branches or projections on the walls and ceilings of their roosts. Their forelimbs, which are used for flight, cannot help support them.

Do animals make homes?

For most people "home" is a settled place where they live, usually with their own family and their possessions. Many animals, from dragonflies to antelopes, live in a "territory." This is an area which contains enough food, water and shelter to enable a pair or group of animals to survive there and rear their young.

A territory may be shared by many other kinds of animal, but not by animals of the same species who would use up the territory's resources. Many mammals mark or spray the territory borders with their scent to warn off intruders.

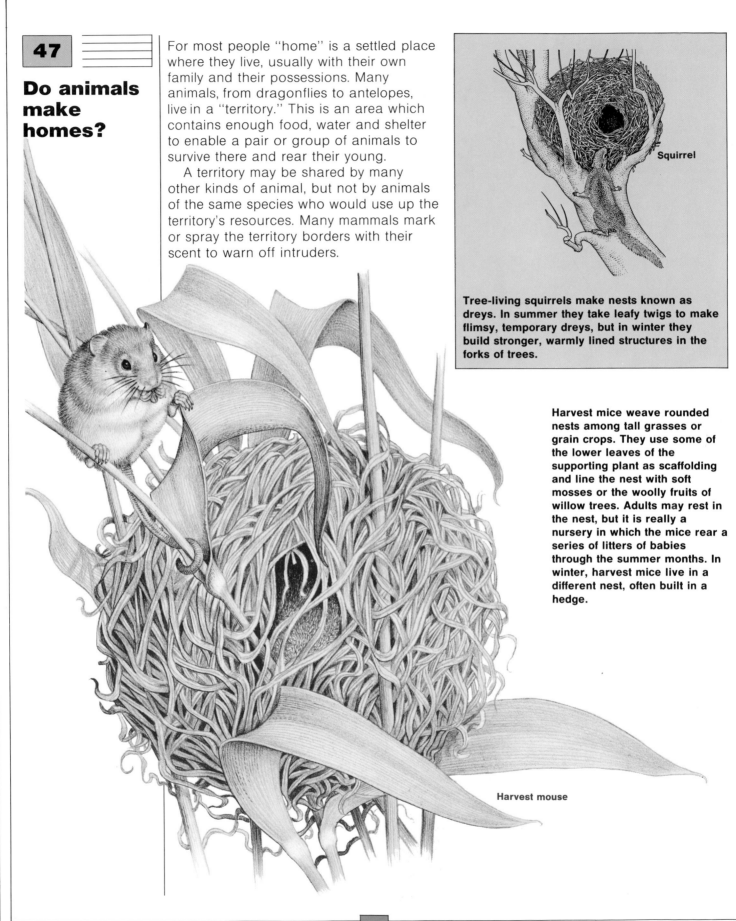

Tree-living squirrels make nests known as dreys. In summer they take leafy twigs to make flimsy, temporary dreys, but in winter they build stronger, warmly lined structures in the forks of trees.

Squirrel

Harvest mice weave rounded nests among tall grasses or grain crops. They use some of the lower leaves of the supporting plant as scaffolding and line the nest with soft mosses or the woolly fruits of willow trees. Adults may rest in the nest, but it is really a nursery in which the mice rear a series of litters of babies through the summer months. In winter, harvest mice live in a different nest, often built in a hedge.

Harvest mouse

Animals such as badgers and prairie dogs live in groups throughout their lives. The places in which they live can be much like human homes.

Prairie dogs live in enormous colonies, or "towns," which may cover several square miles and house several different groups, or coteries, of animals. Each coterie has its own interconnecting burrows, like an apartment within a complex. Other creatures may enter to prey on inhabitants.

When the coterie's quarters become overcrowded, the adult prairie dogs move into new quarters, leaving their burrows to their young. In this way the town's boundaries are expanded.

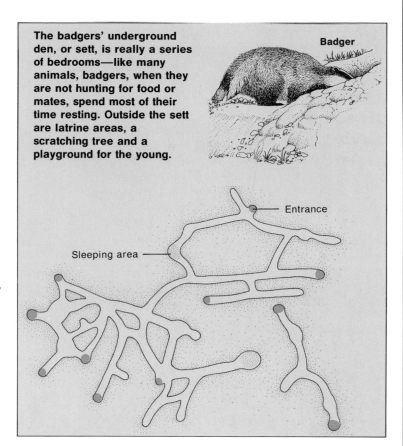

The badgers' underground den, or sett, is really a series of bedrooms—like many animals, badgers, when they are not hunting for food or mates, spend most of their time resting. Outside the sett are latrine areas, a scratching tree and a playground for the young.

Badger

Entrance

Sleeping area

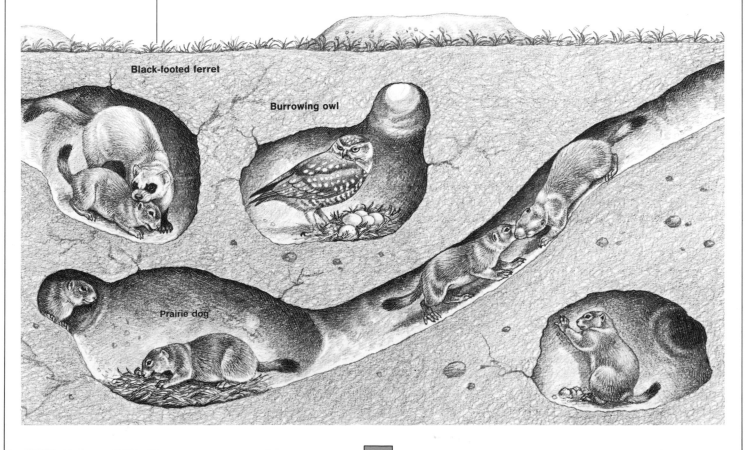

Black-footed ferret

Burrowing owl

Prairie dog

How do animals affect their environment?

All creatures affect their environment just by being alive. Every breath an animal takes alters the balance of oxygen, carbon dioxide and moisture in the air. Every meal that it eats alters the amount of food in its habitat; every time the animal excretes it adds minerals and moisture to its living place.

In natural conditions plants and animals are in balance, each recycling the others' wastes, and numbers of both can stay steady almost indefinitely. Occasionally, one kind of animal increases greatly in numbers, for some reason, and when this happens the environment may be drastically altered. Plants may be grazed down beyond hope of regrowth and other animals may not have enough food or shelter as a result.

In the normal course of life, a few species have dramatic effects on their surroundings. Apart from humans, those that do so most visibly are the beavers. These large rodents, which weigh up to 45 lb (20 kg), always live near water, usually in a valley with a fairly fast-flowing stream. The beavers start their alterations to the habitat by building a dam of stones, lengths of tree trunk, twigs and mud and creating a large, quiet pool. In this they have underwater entries to tunnels in the stream bank, to the living quarters and to food stores in the dam itself. The beavers eat the leaves, twigs and bark of

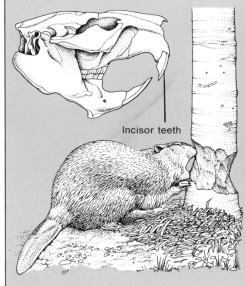

With its huge incisor teeth, a beaver can fell trees up to 3 ft (90 cm) in diameter. The beaver's teeth grow throughout its life and constant gnawing at wood keeps them sharp. The beaver uses its forepaws for holding and manipulating twigs and pushing stones and mud up onto the walls of the dam.

Incisor teeth

Beaver dams may be anything from a few feet to as much as 1,000 ft (300 m) long, but are commonly about 10 ft (3 m) wide and 6 ft (2 m) high.

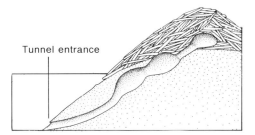

Tunnel entrance

Mud

the trees that they fell; anything inedible is used to strengthen the dam.

Eventually, the beavers remove all the trees within an area of several hundred yards of the stream. When there are no more trees the beavers have no building materials or food and must abandon the site. In time, the pool will silt up and new trees grow on the rich soil left by the beavers' activities. Early settlers in North America liked such land, called beaver meadows, because of its richness. Montreal is built on beaver meadows.

European rabbits can have drastic effects on an area. When they feed they nibble away any plants more than 1 in (2.5 cm) tall, destroying young woody growth and preventing the regrowth of trees and tall plants. Mature trees can also be destroyed when rabbits feed on their bark in winter.

All that is left on land heavily inhabited by rabbits is close cropped, usually grassy, turf, sometimes with low-growing herbs. Annual weeds may dominate in the disturbed earth around the rabbits' warrens—only weeds can survive such unstable conditions. Rabbits came originally from the dry lands of the Iberian Peninsula; they seem to make anywhere they live resemble their desertlike ancestral home.

Rabbit

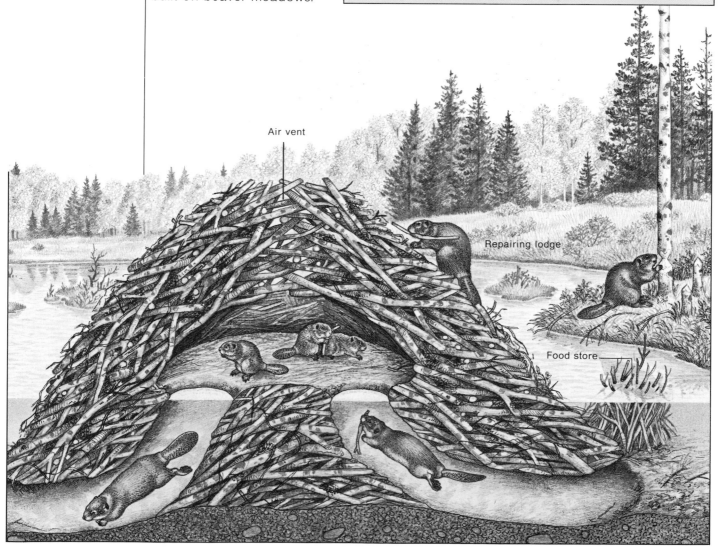

Air vent

Repairing lodge

Food store

Do insects make homes?

Most insects have short lives and do not look after their young, so they do not need to make homes. However, some kinds of bees and wasps lay their eggs in a nest which they stock with food. The larvae never see their mother, but live in the nest until they are adult. Potter wasps, for example, make mud nests which they stock with insects for their young to eat.

The social insects—ants, termites and some kinds of bees and wasps—build elaborate homes which are much more like human communities. In these nests, vast colonies of insects live, dividing the daily tasks among them. Some care for larvae while others repair and enlarge the nest and gather food for the whole colony. The queen, the female on whom the colony centers, is left free for the task of egg laying.

Ants' and termites' nests may house up to a million individuals. The purpose of these nests is to provide protection from enemies and a dark, warm, humid environment. Termites depend enormously on this shelter and cannot survive exposure to the open air for more than a few hours. Their nests may be made in trees, on the ground or underground.

Most dramatic of all insect homes are the giant nests made by some species of plains-dwelling termites. These are made of mud which, when mixed with the saliva of the workers, hardens like concrete when it dries.

The main part of the nest is underground and contains chambers for larvae, larders, and "gardens" where fungi, related to mushrooms and toadstools, are cultivated by the workers for use as food. In the royal cell the queen lives and is tended by workers since she is too fat to move. Many times the size of the worker termites, the queen's sole purpose is to lay eggs and she may produce two million in a year. She is generally accompanied by her mate—termites are the only social insects in which the male lives as long as the female.

Soldier termites defend the queen and her mate and the rest of the colony. They have huge heads and jaws and are bigger than worker termites.

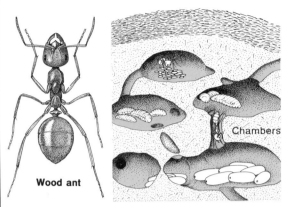

The wood ant is a forest hunter which feeds on many insects among the trees. Its **nest contains nurseries and larder areas for storing the colony's food supplies.**

Wood ant

Chambers

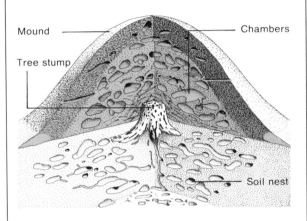

Mound

Tree stump

Chambers

Soil nest

A wood ants' nest, started around a tree stump, quickly outgrows its support. A **nest a yard high above ground extends at least half a yard underground.**

All ants live in colonies and most build nests on or under the ground, or in or around trees and plants. Wood ants make mound nests. They collect tiny particles of soil, twigs, leaves and other vegetation and use them to build up a network of chambers supported by columns. To keep the mound warm inside, the outside is well insulated with a layer of plant material.

The ants keep a constant check on the temperature of the mound, changing the layer of protection to suit the season. Young may be moved to the top of the mound, the warmest place, in the middle of the day and then taken back to chambers lower down at night.

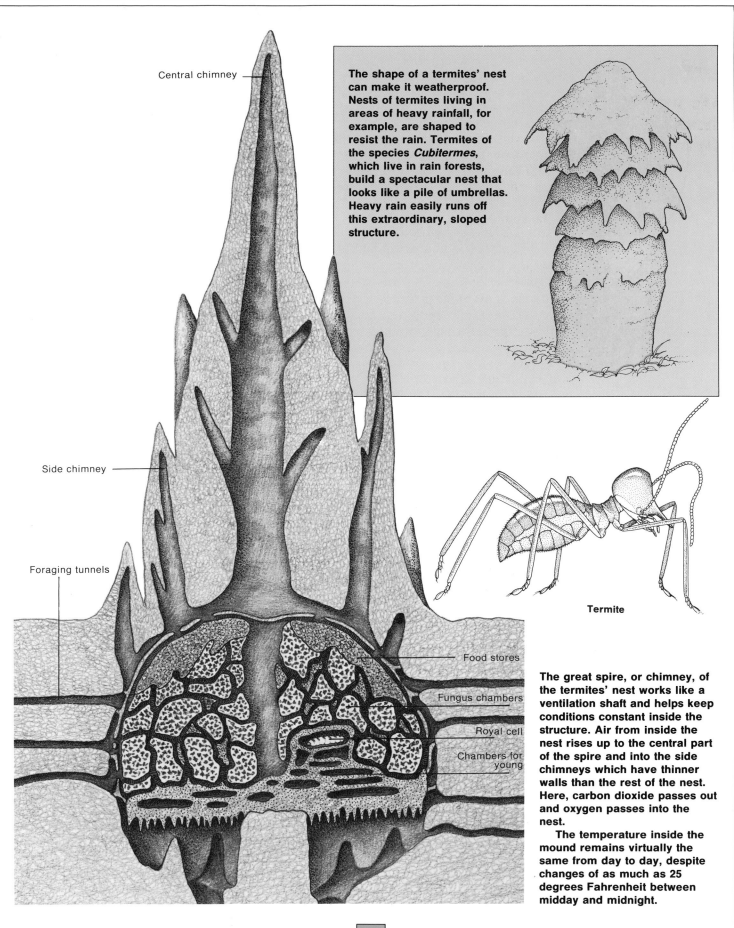

Central chimney

The shape of a termites' nest can make it weatherproof. Nests of termites living in areas of heavy rainfall, for example, are shaped to resist the rain. Termites of the species *Cubitermes*, which live in rain forests, build a spectacular nest that looks like a pile of umbrellas. Heavy rain easily runs off this extraordinary, sloped structure.

Side chimney

Foraging tunnels

Food stores

Fungus chambers

Royal cell

Chambers for young

Termite

The great spire, or chimney, of the termites' nest works like a ventilation shaft and helps keep conditions constant inside the structure. Air from inside the nest rises up to the central part of the spire and into the side chimneys which have thinner walls than the rest of the nest. Here, carbon dioxide passes out and oxygen passes into the nest.

The temperature inside the mound remains virtually the same from day to day, despite changes of as much as 25 degrees Fahrenheit between midday and midnight.

Why and how do bees make honey?

Honey is made from flower nectar. Honeybees store it to feed on during the winter when there are few flowers in bloom. Nectar is a watery solution of sugars, plus a little protein and some salts that are produced by flowering plants to attract pollinating insects. Using tongues shaped like drinking straws, honeybees sip up nectar which passes into the honey stomach, a portion of their gut.

On returning to the nest the bee gives up its load of nectar to a young bee who has not yet started foraging. This bee brings the nectar up onto her tongue, then swallows it again, repeating the action 80 or more times in the next 20 minutes. During this process, much of the water in the nectar evaporates and sucrose, the complex sugar it contains, is broken down into simpler sugars. The half-ripe honey is stored in a cell, then later worked on again. When the water is sufficiently reduced, the honey is ready to be stored.

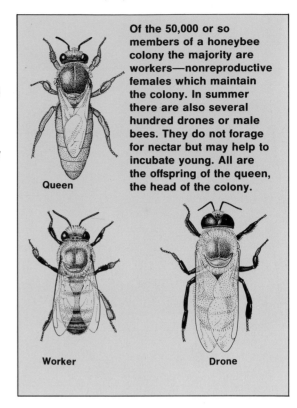

Of the 50,000 or so members of a honeybee colony the majority are workers—nonreproductive females which maintain the colony. In summer there are also several hundred drones or male bees. They do not forage for nectar but may help to incubate young. All are the offspring of the queen, the head of the colony.

Queen

Worker

Drone

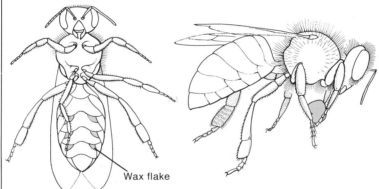

Wax flake

The honeybees' nest is made of wax, formed in glands on the abdomens of workers early in their adult lives. The worker scrapes the flakes of wax into a ball and works it with her jaws, adding saliva to give it flexibility. She can then use the wax to build the thin-walled hexagonal cells which pack together to form the nest, or to repair or enlarge the comb.

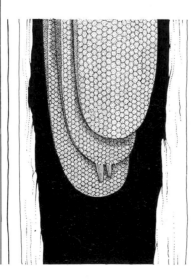

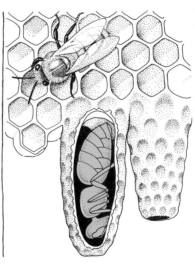

The nest may be made in a natural cavity, such as a hollow tree, or in a hive provided for the bees. The vertical slabs of cells it contains are known as combs. The cells house stores of pollen, which is fed to the young, or honey. In the warmest part of the nest is the brood area where the queen lays her eggs. Cells containing developing males are on the edge of the main brood area. Larger cells, holding young destined to become queens, are often on the lower edges of the comb.

Not all bees make honey. Many lead short solitary lives and obtain all the nourishment they need from flowers. Some species of bee which provide food for their young may add slightly altered nectar to supplies of pollen, but true honey is made only by social bees, including bumble bees, which live as a colony with a queen and workers.

Only the honeybees make honey in large quantities. Although the life of an individual worker may be short, the colony is long lived and food must be stored to last its members through the winter.

Honeybees make enormous quantities of honey. In a good year a beekeeper may obtain over 88 lb (40 kg) from one hive. This honey must be replaced with sugar or the bees will starve.

Worker honeybee

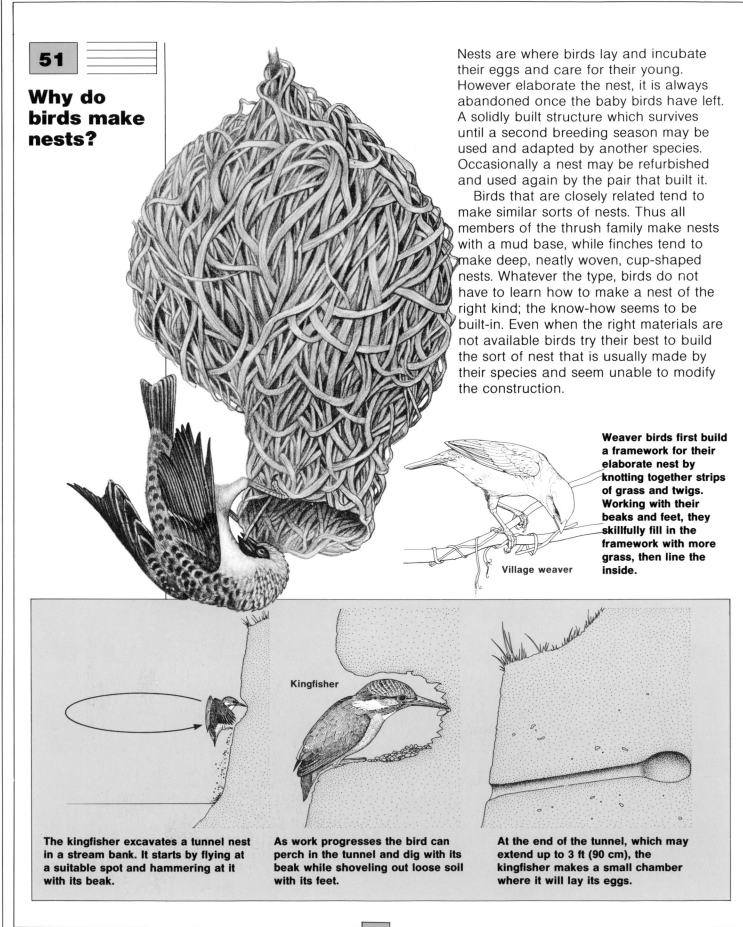

51

Why do birds make nests?

Nests are where birds lay and incubate their eggs and care for their young. However elaborate the nest, it is always abandoned once the baby birds have left. A solidly built structure which survives until a second breeding season may be used and adapted by another species. Occasionally a nest may be refurbished and used again by the pair that built it.

Birds that are closely related tend to make similar sorts of nests. Thus all members of the thrush family make nests with a mud base, while finches tend to make deep, neatly woven, cup-shaped nests. Whatever the type, birds do not have to learn how to make a nest of the right kind; the know-how seems to be built-in. Even when the right materials are not available birds try their best to build the sort of nest that is usually made by their species and seem unable to modify the construction.

Weaver birds first build a framework for their elaborate nest by knotting together strips of grass and twigs. Working with their beaks and feet, they skillfully fill in the framework with more grass, then line the inside.

Village weaver

Kingfisher

The kingfisher excavates a tunnel nest in a stream bank. It starts by flying at a suitable spot and hammering at it with its beak.

As work progresses the bird can perch in the tunnel and dig with its beak while shoveling out loose soil with its feet.

At the end of the tunnel, which may extend up to 3 ft (90 cm), the kingfisher makes a small chamber where it will lay its eggs.

Where do birds make their nests?

Birds make nests anywhere that provides safety from predators and bad weather. Many use the cover of trees or other tall plants, but others, such as skylarks, make well camouflaged nests on the ground.

Where the nest is made often influences what it is made of. Twigs, grass and moss are used by birds that nest in trees or hedges. Other birds, including many swallows, use mud to make nests but none so expertly as the South American ovenbirds, which make a thick-walled "room," often on a fence post. Cave swiftlets make nests of hardened saliva.

Woodpeckers and hornbills are among the many birds that nest in holes in trees. Some hornbills make sure their eggs are safe by walling up the nest and female. At the other extreme, many sea birds simply lay their eggs in a dip on the ground.

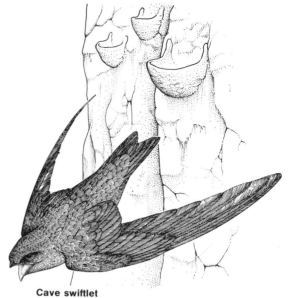

Cave swiftlet

Ovenbird

Little tern

Skylark

Great Indian hornbill

53

Why do birds lay eggs?

A bird's body is a sort of flying machine and, like an airplane, must avoid excess weight to stay airborne. A female bird, about to produce young, would be too heavily burdened to fly if she were to carry the total weight of her developing brood inside her as a mammal does.

To solve this weight problem, birds lay eggs with large yolks, which nourish the developing young. Birds that lay a clutch of more than one egg, lay one a day or one every other day. This means that the mother has a single fast-growing egg inside her at any one time. Even a tiny bird such as a wren can lay a clutch of seven or eight eggs, the total heavier than her own weight, without being grounded.

Coot

54

Which bird lays the biggest egg?

Of all living birds the ostrich lays the biggest eggs. Each one is about 6 in (15 cm) long, 5 in (12.5 cm) at its greatest width and weighs about 3½ lb (1.6 kg). The smallest egg is laid by a hummingbird, the short-tailed woodstar. This egg is ⅓ in (1 cm) long, ¼ in (6 mm) wide and weighs 0.01 oz (0.3 g).

As a rule the smaller the bird, the smaller its egg, but the greater the proportion of its weight to the weight of the bird. The eggs of many hummingbirds are 25 percent of their body weight, while an ostrich's egg is only 1.7 percent of its body weight. One unusual example is the kiwi of New Zealand. A large—but flightless—bird, it produces an egg which is 25 percent of its body weight.

Hummingbird 0.07 oz (2 g)
Egg 0.018 oz (0.5 g)
25% of body weight

Kiwi 3 lb 12 oz (1.7 kg)
Egg 14.8 oz (420 g)
25% of body weight

Wren 0.29 oz (8.15 g)
Egg 0.037 oz (1.06 g)
13% of body weight

Golden-fronted woodpecker
0.74 oz (21 g) Egg 0.07 oz (2.1 g)
10% of body weight

Cuckoo 5 oz (142 g)
Egg 0.165 oz (4.6 g)
3.3% of body weight

Ostrich 214 lb (97 kg)
Egg 3 lb 11 oz (1.6 kg)
1.7% of body weight

55

Why do birds sit on their eggs?

A new laid egg needs to be kept warm, or incubated, if it is to develop. The best way for the parent bird to provide this warmth is to sit on the eggs, keeping them at a temperature close to its own.

The length of time a bird incubates its egg varies from 11 to 14 days for small songbirds to about 80 for the royal albatross. As a rule, birds that lay large eggs which hatch into active young incubate them for longer than birds that produce helpless young from small eggs.

Flightless cormorants

56

How is an egg made?

An egg starts as a yolky cell, the oocyte, in the ovary of a hen bird. The oocyte breaks free and enters a tube, the oviduct, where it is fertilized by a sperm which has traveled up the oviduct after mating.

As the fertilized ovum passes down the oviduct the egg white, or albumen, is added in four separate layers, some thin and some thick. Between them these layers protect the yolk and its developing embryo. Twisted ropes of albumen, the chalazae, lie along the length of the egg and stabilize the yolk when it is turned during incubation. This ensures that the growing embryo is always in the position of maximum warmth.

The inner and outer shell membranes are formed in a lower part of the oviduct, the isthmus. Finally, in the lowest part of all, the uterus, the shell itself is formed and given color. The air space develops only after the egg is laid and is thought to help conserve the water within the egg.

A bird's eggs originate as oocytes in the left ovary or egg-producing organ. A newly hatched bird contains about 1,000,000 oocytes, most of which die during growth. In the breeding season hormone changes cause the bird's liver to produce the yolk, a mixture of proteins and fats, which provides food for the developing embryo.

Ovary

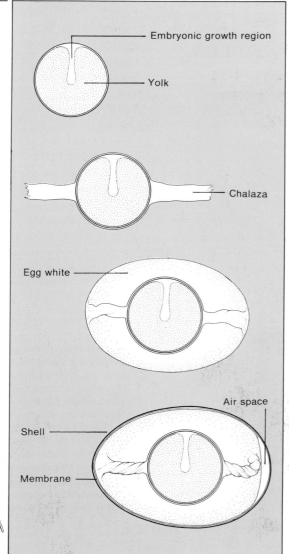

Embryonic growth region

Yolk

Chalaza

Egg white

Air space

Shell

Membrane

Are newborn baby animals as helpless as human babies?

Many animal babies are just as much in need of care and protection at birth as human babies but others, such as giraffe and zebras, can be standing up within minutes.

Animals that are helpless at birth are generally born in a protected nest, or some place where they are safe from bad weather and enemies. This may be an underground burrow or a well-hidden lair. Most small mammals, such as mice, rats and hedgehogs, give birth after a short gestation—the period of the baby's growth inside the mother. These animals must complete their development after they have been born.

The largest animals to give birth to helpless young are bears. Although their mother may weigh several hundred pounds, bear cubs weigh only a few ounces. They are born in midwinter in a den, but do not emerge from this safe home until they are several months old.

Large, plant-eating, plains-dwelling creatures give birth to active young. Almost all produce one baby after a long gestation period. The offspring are quick to run and feed on solid food, although they may continue to suckle milk from their mother for several months.

The young of whales and dolphins are most active of all—they must swim alongside their mothers from the moment of birth. They are also the largest of all babies in comparison to the mother's size: a newborn baby porpoise weighs 11 to 13 lb (5–6 kg) and measures half its mother's length of about 5 ft (1.5 m).

Hare

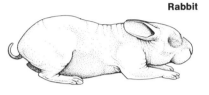

Rabbit

Closely related animals may produce young that vary widely in the amount they are developed. A baby rabbit, born underground in a warm nest, is tiny, naked and blind at birth. Born above ground, the leveret, offspring of the hare, is fully furred, has its eyes open and can nibble grass when only a few days old.

Monkey

Although otherwise helpless and dependent on their parents, the babies of primates such as monkeys, chimpanzees and gorillas have powerful hands and toes with which they can cling to their mothers from birth. They stay with their mothers for at least one year, or up to three years in larger species.

Ducks, waders and sea birds are among the birds that lay large eggs from which well-grown chicks hatch. The lapwing chick, which hatches after 28 days, is downy, open-eyed and can walk and peck almost at once—a state termed "precocial." The blackbird, like most songbirds, lays small eggs which hatch after 14 days. The chick is "altricial"—it is blind, naked and helpless and needs to be fed and warmed by its parents.

Blackbird   Lapwing

Zebra

A zebra mare about to produce a foal is guarded by her mate who stands within 43 yds (40 m) of her as she lies down to give birth. Within three minutes of being clear of its mother's body, the foal makes its first attempt to stand, although it may not succeed immediately. The mother licks her foal to help it learn to recognize her by smell.

Within fifteen minutes of the birth, the mare stands up and she and her foal walk slowly to join the other members of the herd. She may soon begin to graze again.

An hour after its birth the foal has found its mother's teats and taken its first feed of milk. It suckles for at least six months, but also starts to eat grass when a few days old. It stays close by its mother's side and does not make contact with other members of the herd for several days, by which time it has learned to recognize its mother. The young zebra remains with its mother for about a year.

58

Do animals feed their young?

All mammals, many birds and even some fish and insects feed their young, even if only for a brief period. Young mammals first feed by sucking milk from their mothers. Some, such as the young of grazing animals, soon start to find their own food by following the parents' example. Others—lions, wolves, and monkeys, for example—are brought food by the parents for many months.

Many invertebrates, animals without backbones, die before their young hatch. They lay eggs which provide the developing young with food, but they cannot care for their families directly. A few species, particularly social insects such as termites and bees (see p 54), do provide food supplies for their young.

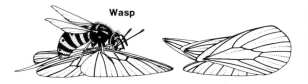

Wasp

Worker wasps are kept busy hunting food for their young. They kill other insects, such as flies and butterflies, which they carry back to their nest. They may remove the victims' wings, which cannot be eaten, to lighten their burden.

The young of perching birds, birds of prey, sea birds and many others are fed by their parents until they can fend for themselves. Ducks, hens and plovers are among the birds which must start scratching around for their own food right away.

The mothers of young mammals all feed their babies on their own milk at first. The milk contains all the proteins, fats, sugars and vitamins vital to early growth. The young suck the milk from the mother's nipples or teats. Animals such as pigs and dogs, which produce large litters, have many nipples. Female primates, elephants and horses, which bear one or two young, have only one pair.

Pig

Do any male animals provide the food for their young?

In many, but not all, kinds of animals males do help to feed and care for their young. Males of perching birds, birds of prey and many others work hard at bringing food—the demands of the hungry young would probably be too much for one parent. Male help is rarer in mammals but, after the initial period of suckling from the mother, some, such as male wolves and foxes, help to find food for the young.

In just a few species the males play an even more crucial part. Male sea horses and pipe fish take charge of the eggs laid by their mate and carry them in a brood pouch on the underside of their bodies. Pigeons are unique in that both males and females produce a milklike substance on which the young feed for the first four days of their lives.

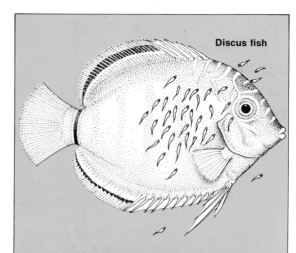

Discus fish

Discus fish—both male and female—feed their young on slime produced by their own skin. Their eggs are laid in gravel and the newly hatched young moved to water plants. At about three days, the young can swim to their parents and start to feed.

Pigeon

Crop

Specially thickened areas of the pigeon's crop—an extension of the windpipe usually used for food storage—produce a thick secretion, similar to a mammal's milk.

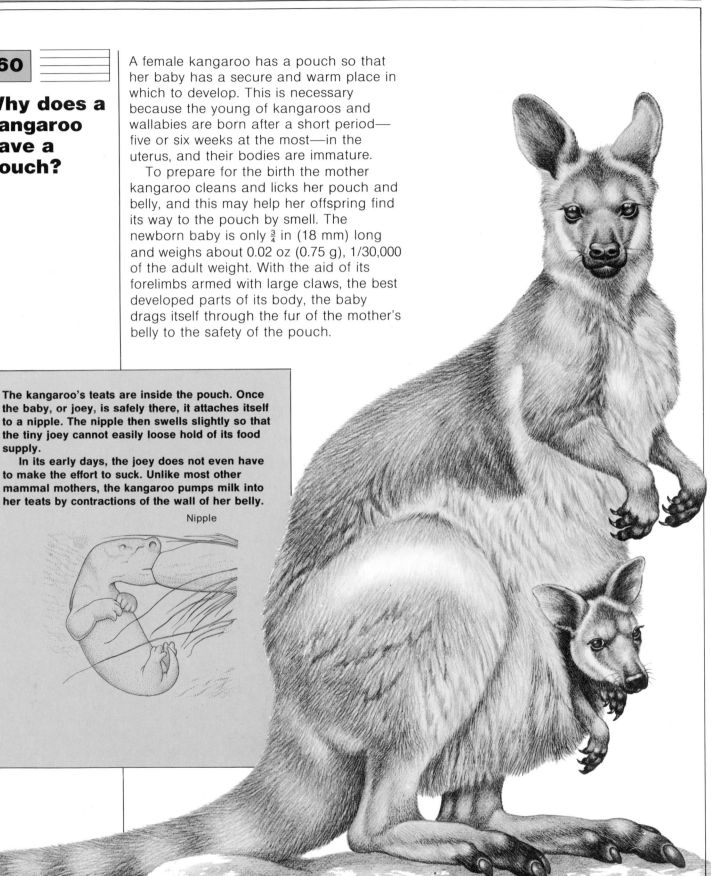

60

Why does a kangaroo have a pouch?

A female kangaroo has a pouch so that her baby has a secure and warm place in which to develop. This is necessary because the young of kangaroos and wallabies are born after a short period—five or six weeks at the most—in the uterus, and their bodies are immature.

To prepare for the birth the mother kangaroo cleans and licks her pouch and belly, and this may help her offspring find its way to the pouch by smell. The newborn baby is only $\frac{3}{4}$ in (18 mm) long and weighs about 0.02 oz (0.75 g), 1/30,000 of the adult weight. With the aid of its forelimbs armed with large claws, the best developed parts of its body, the baby drags itself through the fur of the mother's belly to the safety of the pouch.

The kangaroo's teats are inside the pouch. Once the baby, or joey, is safely there, it attaches itself to a nipple. The nipple then swells slightly so that the tiny joey cannot easily loose hold of its food supply.

In its early days, the joey does not even have to make the effort to suck. Unlike most other mammal mothers, the kangaroo pumps milk into her teats by contractions of the wall of her belly.

Nipple

Ring-tailed wallaby

61

How long does a baby kangaroo stay in its mother's pouch?

The journey to its mother's pouch takes the joey two minutes at most, but it remains there for a long period—ten months in the great grey kangaroo, a year in the red kangaroo. At the end of this time the joey is big enough to live outside the mother, but is suckled by her for up to another six months.

Even a well-grown joey will return to the pouch when threatened, leaping in headfirst and turning itself around as its mother speeds away from danger.

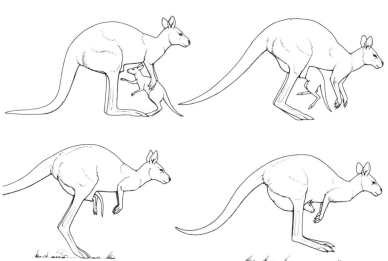

62

Do any other animals have pouches?

Kangaroos are not the only pouched mammals. They belong to a group of about 250 species known as marsupials, all of which give birth to minute young. The marsupials are not all like kangaroos—in their ways of life and appearance they parallel and resemble other more familiar mammals. There are marsupials which look like mice, moles, monkeys (the cuscuses) and flying squirrels (flying possums).

The young of all pouched mammals are fed on milk for a long period, almost always in the shelter of a pouch. Most of the world's marsupials live in Australasia but there are about 80 species of opossum in South America, and the Virginia opossum is found as far north as the Canadian border.

The spiny anteater is not a pouched mammal but an egg-layer. However, its egg is laid directly into a protective pouch which forms temporarily on the female's belly. Once hatched, the baby finds the milk supply within the pouch and remains there until the growth of its spines makes it an unwelcome tenant.

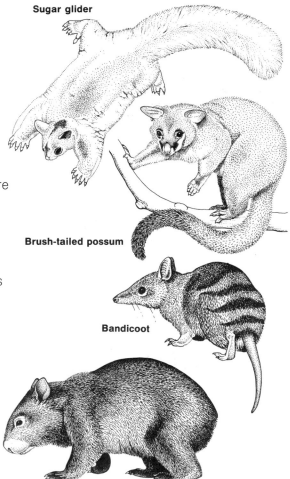

Sugar glider

Brush-tailed possum

Bandicoot

Spiny anteater

Wombat

63

Are animal families like ours?

All animals have young but only birds and mammals have families like those of human beings and care for their babies for any length of time. The babies of these animals are kept warm and safe, often in a nest or den. They are fed by their parents and also learn many things from them.

Most creatures grow up much faster than humans. A fox cub, for example, lives with its parents for several months but is adult at a year old. Human beings and the great apes, such as gorillas and chimpanzees, have a longer childhood during which they are dependent on their parents. In growing up slowly they have time to learn how to make the best of the world in which they live.

Insects and other invertebrates do not usually care directly for their young. Many have such short lives that the parents die before the next generation hatch from their eggs. But most do their best for the offspring by laying eggs in sheltered places or near a plentiful supply of food.

Baboons live in groups, usually of about 50 animals. Of these seven or eight will be males, twice that number adult females and the rest babies and young animals. The males usually lead the troop.

Baby baboons are black for the first weeks of life. This makes them conspicuous and extremely interesting to the rest of the troop, who try to touch and fondle new arrivals. The babies quickly learn to recognize all members of the troop and grow up well integrated with the whole family.

Baboons

Lions generally live in a family group, or pride. This includes several adult males, a larger number of females, and cubs, some of which may be nearly fully grown. The cubs stay close to their mothers for the first two months of life. They then begin to explore and meet other pride members, who are extremely tolerant of their playfulness. Cubs are suckled for about eight months. Unlike most other creatures, lionesses will feed babies other than their own. Young lions start to join hunting expeditions when about a year old but are usually over three before they become really expert hunters.

Lion pride

64

Do all animals play?

Mammals, particularly the young of larger species such as lions and chimps, do commonly play. Some birds also appear to do so, but it is far less usual. Invertebrates, animals without backbones, are not known to play, nor are fish, amphibians or reptiles.

Play is activity done for its own sake and not immediately concerned with survival. Although an animal may play on its own, often with an object, play is usually social. Among the more intelligent creatures, particularly monkeys, apes and the carnivores such as cats and dogs, adults as well as young play. Less intelligent creatures, such as sheep and horses, tend to play only when young.

Monkey   Chimpanzee

Rough play can easily seem like fighting, so some animals use special "play invitation" actions or expressions to make their intentions clear. A chimp may approach a playmate with an open-mouthed smile. A young monkey may look through its legs as a sign that it wants to play.

Rhesus monkeys

Why do animals play?

Badgers play all through their lives, but cubs, which do not have to use their energy looking for food, are particularly fun-loving. When they first start to come out of their burrow they stay close to mother. Once they have more confidence their play is active and noisy, usually involving mock battles of various kinds. Badgers may play biting games, grabbing the opponent's head, ears or tail, or try to turn each other over by butting movements of the head.

Badger

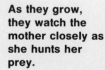

Lion

Play gets rid of surplus energy in a harmless way but also helps a young animal develop and perfect its coordination. For some animals, particularly the young of flesh-eating species like cats and dogs, play is part of their education. Adult foxes bring disabled prey to their young so they can practice the actions necessary for making a kill. Fighting games with brothers and sisters teach a cub the forms of attack and defense which may be vital in later life.

Young animals usually play with their equals in age and build so nobody gets seriously hurt. An adult animal about to play with a younger one adopts a posture to show that it means no harm.

Up to three months, baby cheetahs play together, watched by their mother.

As they grow, they watch the mother closely as she hunts her prey.

By seven months, a cub follows its mother on the hunt and may try a kill.

A year old cheetah, strengthened by play and practice, may start to hunt on its own.

How do animals protect themselves?

Animals protect themselves by their behavior—they may simply run or hide from danger—or by their structure. The life of any animal is a constant battle against danger. Animal enemies need not be living—storms, cold and other harsh weather can kill many creatures. Those that survive the cold have thick fur to protect them, or can build up supplies of fat to tide them over food shortages.

Hedgehogs are among the creatures that avoid winter's hardships by hibernating (see p 40). Many birds and mammals, and even some insects, regularly migrate long distances to find better weather or food supplies (see p 42).

Creatures must also protect themselves against those who hunt them to feed on their flesh. Some do this by being camouflaged, which makes them hard for predators to find. Others are safe because they are so big they are difficult to overcome—few predators attack adult elephants or rhinos.

Hatpin urchin

Hatpin sea urchins, found in shallow tropical seas, have long sharp poisonous spines, which are slightly barbed at the tips. If a creature brushes against them, the spines break off and work into the flesh of the intruder, causing great pain. Most animals are careful to avoid these urchins.

The giant armadillo of the tropical South American forests is armored against all enemies—except for humans. Its body is covered with a mosaic of small bones set in its skin.

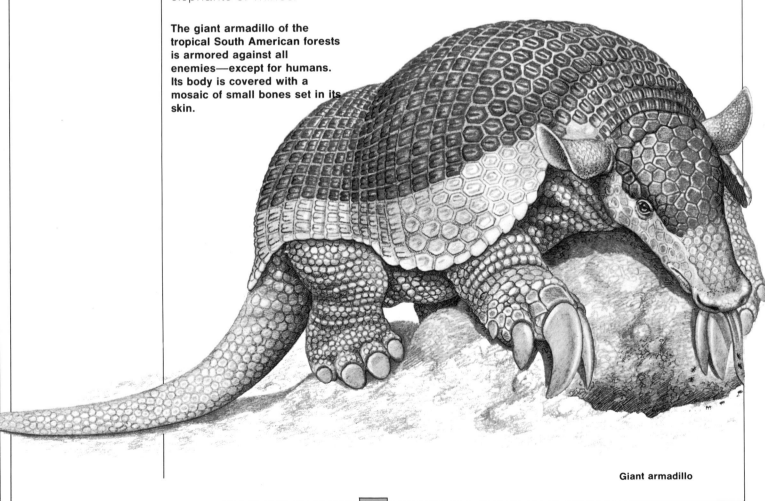

Giant armadillo

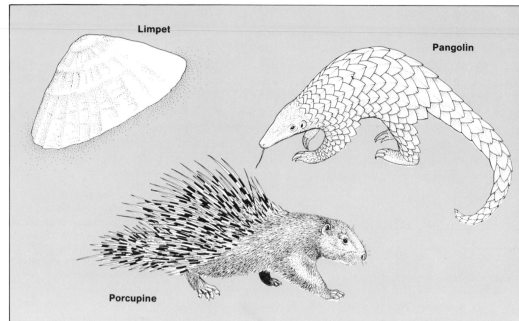

Limpet

Pangolin

Porcupine

Animal armor is wonderfully varied. The limpet, like almost all mollusks, carries a shell made of layers of calcium salts and proteins. This protects it from predators, and from the effects of the battering waves, the sun and the wind. The porcupine has spines which are really huge hairs. Long and sharp, the spines are offputting to enemies but, because they are hollow, are lighter than most armor. The pangolin's scales are made of thick layers of keratin, the material of which skin and fingernails are made.

Ladybirds and many other insects taste nasty and advertise the fact with their bright colors which enemies learn to avoid. Biting, stinging and forms of chemical attack are among the effective forms of defense used by insects, fish and jellyfish.

Creatures ranging from beetles, crabs and snails to tortoises and mammals such as armadillos and pangolins carry their own armor as protection. The armor is made of shell, bone or spines and strong enough to defy the teeth and claws of that animal's enemies.

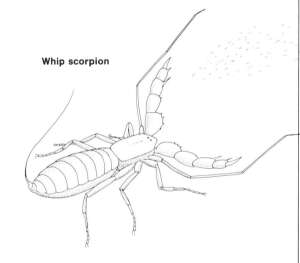

Whip scorpion

The whip scorpion, a relative of the spiders and true scorpions, defends itself with a chemical produced in a gland in its tail. If attacked, the scorpion sprays its enemy with this unpleasant fluid—acetic acid. Ants make acid in their bodies with which to protect themselves; if attacked, they can squirt acid at the enemy. In some kinds of ants, the acid accounts for a third of their body weight.

Eland

Many plant-eating animals, including antelopes, deer and goats, are armed with horns or antlers and sharp hooves with which they attempt to drive off predators. In many of these species only the adult males have horns—the rest find safety in numbers by living in large herds. Hunters will almost always try to isolate one member of the herd when making a kill.

67

Do animals talk to each other?

Almost all animals have some way of communicating with others of their own kind. Some have a definite vocabulary of distinctive sounds. Small finches and titmice may make up to 25 different calls with which they inform each other of the presence of food or enemies; they have different calls to warn of predators on the ground and in the air. Many other creatures, such as squirrels and monkeys, also have a range of warning sounds which communicate different meanings.

Whales and dolphins are thought to have an intricate language. Some scientists believe these animals hold conversations which are similar to human chatter, but there is not yet any proof of this. Probably only humans hold conversations in which ideas are exchanged. Animals cannot make sounds as subtle as human speech nor express abstract thoughts.

Animals of the same group or family may seem to be talking. The noises they make are usually small sounds of affection or reassurance.

Chimpanzees

How else do animals communicate?

Smell is probably the most common and basic means of animal communication. Even primitive animals seem sensitive to odors given off by animals of their own and other species. Animals use scents to announce their readiness to mate or to give other social information; for example, they may mark the borders of their home area with strong smelling substances, such as urine, to warn off intruders.

Sight is also important. Many animals have a language of gesture, signaling simple messages with their tails, limbs or with particular feathers. The fiddler crab "waves" to a potential mate with its claws; courting lizards nod their heads in a special way. Others, such as horses, hold their ears or tails in certain positions to show that they are alarmed or pleased.

Touch is sometimes used in communicating, generally in courtship or between parents and their young. Bees use touch in the hive to pass on complex information about the whereabouts of food. A worker bee returning from a good food supply dances on the vertical face of the hive's comb. As she circles and waggles her abdomen she is closely followed by other workers, who constantly touch her. By the direction of movements, and the number of turns of the dance she performs, she can communicate the direction and distance of the food supply.

Mandarin duck

When courting a mate the male mandarin duck uses his elaborate plumage to signal his intentions. As well as his beautiful crest the mandarin has a huge sail-like feather on the upper part of each wing. This feather is held erect in all stages of the display and the male may point toward it as part of his courtship ritual. He may also pretend to preen, dip his beak into water and make special calls as part of his courtship. Groups of drakes display together to females. The female ducks choose the mates who "speak" to them most effectively in their language of gesture and sound.

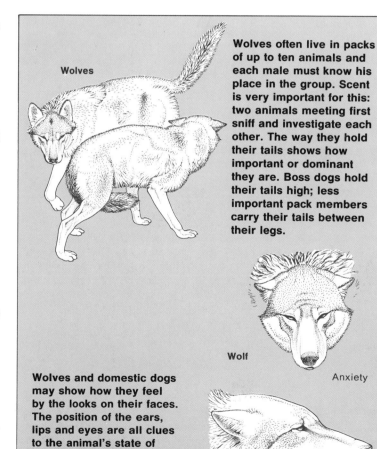

Wolves

Wolves often live in packs of up to ten animals and each male must know his place in the group. Scent is very important for this: two animals meeting first sniff and investigate each other. The way they hold their tails shows how important or dominant they are. Boss dogs hold their tails high; less important pack members carry their tails between their legs.

Wolf

Anxiety

Suspicion

Wolves and domestic dogs may show how they feel by the looks on their faces. The position of the ears, lips and eyes are all clues to the animal's state of mind. An anxious dog and a suspicious dog wear very different expressions.

How does a bee or wasp sting?

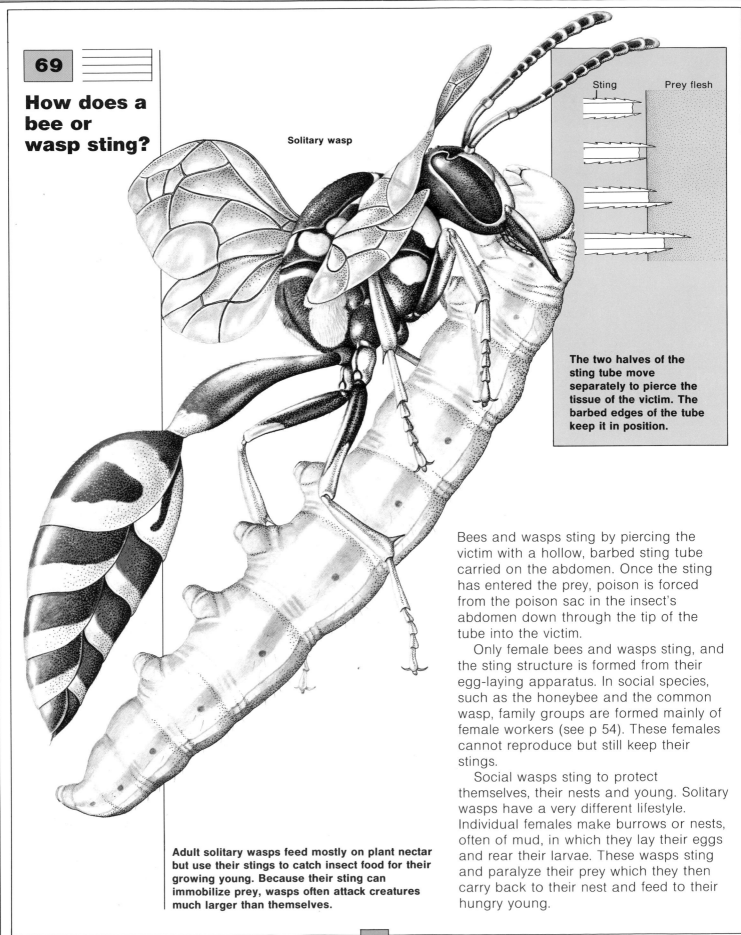

Solitary wasp

Sting   Prey flesh

The two halves of the sting tube move separately to pierce the tissue of the victim. The barbed edges of the tube keep it in position.

Adult solitary wasps feed mostly on plant nectar but use their stings to catch insect food for their growing young. Because their sting can immobilize prey, wasps often attack creatures much larger than themselves.

Bees and wasps sting by piercing the victim with a hollow, barbed sting tube carried on the abdomen. Once the sting has entered the prey, poison is forced from the poison sac in the insect's abdomen down through the tip of the tube into the victim.

Only female bees and wasps sting, and the sting structure is formed from their egg-laying apparatus. In social species, such as the honeybee and the common wasp, family groups are formed mainly of female workers (see p 54). These females cannot reproduce but still keep their stings.

Social wasps sting to protect themselves, their nests and young. Solitary wasps have a very different lifestyle. Individual females make burrows or nests, often of mud, in which they lay their eggs and rear their larvae. These wasps sting and paralyze their prey which they then carry back to their nest and feed to their hungry young.

How does a scorpion sting?

A scorpion stings by injecting poison from a gland at the rear of its body into the prey, which it captures and holds in the heavy pincers on its front limbs. The poison seems to affect the nervous system, immobilizing the victim, then breaking down its tissues.

Both male and female scorpions sting and may do so out of fright or in self-defense as well as to catch food. Some species have venom powerful enough to be fatal even to humans.

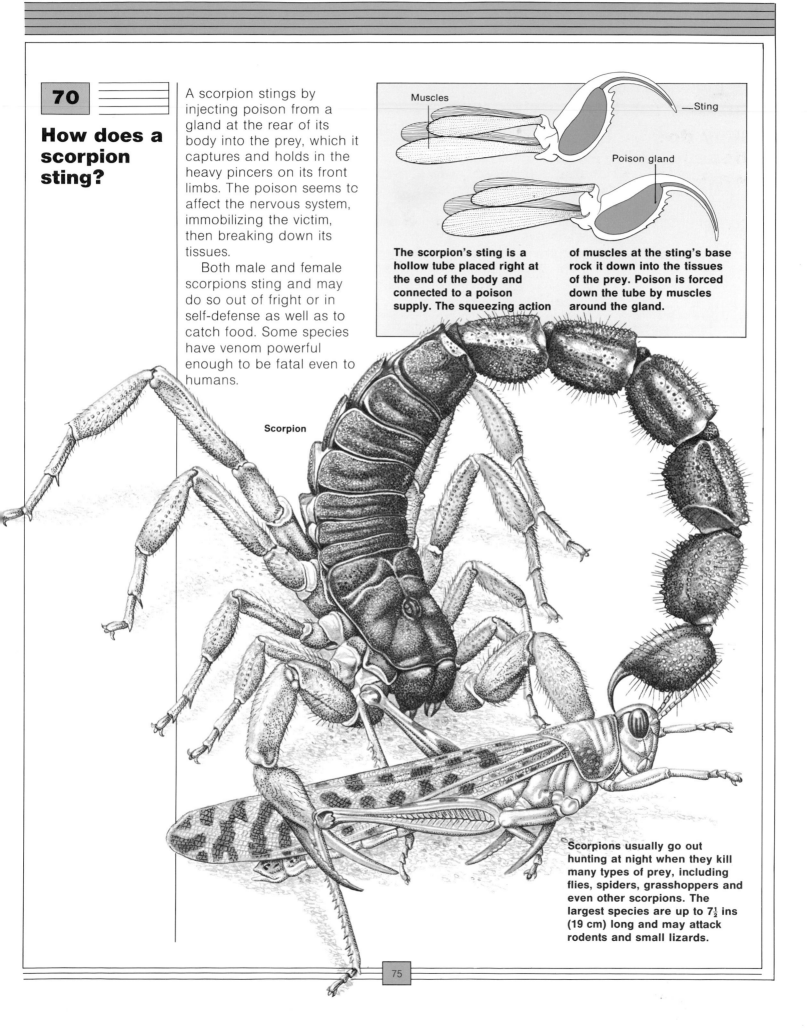

Muscles

Sting

Poison gland

The scorpion's sting is a hollow tube placed right at the end of the body and connected to a poison supply. The squeezing action of muscles at the sting's base rock it down into the tissues of the prey. Poison is forced down the tube by muscles around the gland.

Scorpion

Scorpions usually go out hunting at night when they kill many types of prey, including flies, spiders, grasshoppers and even other scorpions. The largest species are up to $7\frac{1}{2}$ ins (19 cm) long and may attack rodents and small lizards.

Why do fleas jump?

Fleas are parasites and jump in order to get up onto an animal host and feed on its blood. They cannot fly since they have no wings—wings large enough for flight would get in the way as the flea crept through the fur or feathers of its host.

Young (larval) fleas do not live on other animals but in their dens or nests, feeding on scraps of skin or other debris. Once adult, the flea must find a host—a mammal or bird to live on and feed from. The flea senses when such a creature is near by its warmth, and also probably by its smell, and must seize the opportunity to leap up onto it.

There may be only a second or so while the animal passes by for the flea to make the jump which makes the difference between food and life, and starvation and death—hence the importance of its jumping ability.

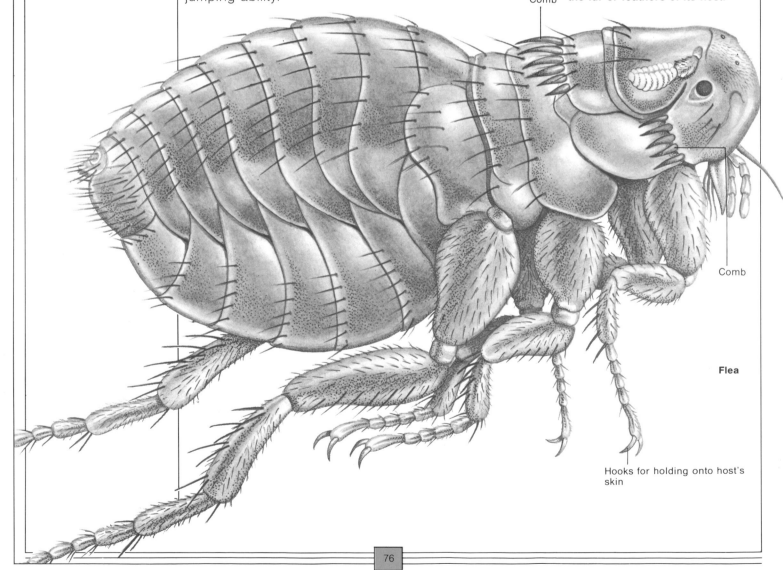

Reselin

Muscles

Hind leg

The power pack for the flea's jump is a small amount of a protein substance called reselin. This is like super-elastic which can store energy when contracted and release it almost instantly when stretched.

Backward-pointing hairs on the flea's body and combs around its head help it stay lodged in the fur or feathers of its host.

Comb

Comb

Flea

Hooks for holding onto host's skin

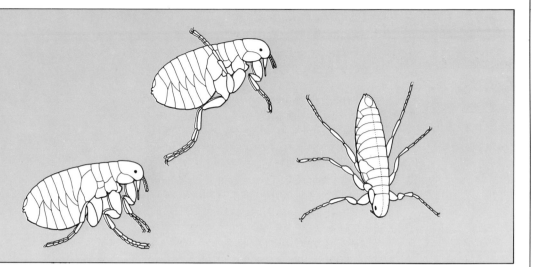

Most fleas can leap over 300 times their own length and can continue jumping for long periods. A rat flea was once observed jumping 600 times an hour for 72 hours—43,200 jumps in all. The fleas which jump the farthest are those with the biggest, most active hosts.

A flea often turns a somersault in the course of a jump. It usually carries one pair of legs above itself; this helps it balance and also allows it to grab on tight once it makes contact with a suitable host.

72

How do animals get rid of parasites?

A mammal or bird can often rid itself of fleas by scratching or nibbling at its fur or feathers. Although the flea takes only a small amount of blood when it feeds, the host finds its bite is itchy and irritating and will try hard to remove the parasite. Picking out fleas is an important part of the grooming which almost all animals spend time on. In social animals like baboons, individuals which are related or friendly may show their closeness by grooming each other.

Some kinds of fleas live and feed only on one type of host: there are rat fleas, rabbit fleas, and so on. Others will feed on the blood of a range of creatures but live on only one kind.

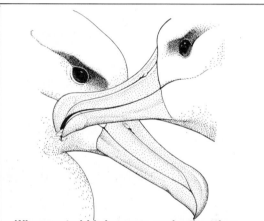

When mated birds preen each other they often clean the feathers of the head and face which they cannot reach for themselves.

Vervet monkeys

Monkeys and apes seem to find great comfort in being groomed. A dominant animal will often be groomed by a more humble member of a group, or friends will groom each other in turn. The groomer combs through the other's fur with its fingers, and pulls out pieces of dirt and fleas. Ticks and mites are removed with the teeth—these blood suckers can become embedded in the animal's skin so need to be removed with care. Grooming behavior has the bonus of cementing the bonds of friendship between the two animals.

73

How are spiders different from insects?

Spiders are not insects. Although they are often confused with them, they differ from them in many ways. Most adult insects, for example, have wings; spiders never do. All insects have bodies divided into three major parts: head, thorax and abdomen, the latter two divided into smaller segments. The thorax carries four or six legs, never more. A spider's body is in two main parts. Attached to the front one of these are eight legs, never fewer.

Baby spiders hatch out of eggs as tiny versions of their parents. They never undergo a stage as larvae or caterpillars as many insects do. Many adult insects have large complex eyes and can see quite well. Spiders usually have small eyes and most are probably short-sighted. Many insects feed on plants, but all spiders are hunters which catch and eat other creatures.

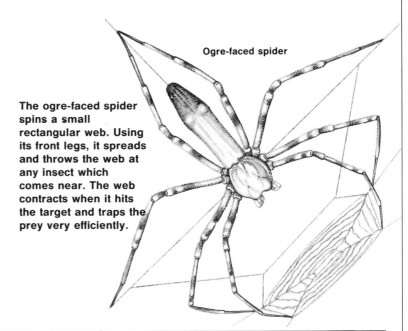

Spitting spider

The spitting spider squirts sticky threads, produced by glands in the front part of the body, at its prey. These threads fix the prey to the ground so that it is unable to escape.

Ogre-faced spider

The ogre-faced spider spins a small rectangular web. Using its front legs, it spreads and throws the web at any insect which comes near. The web contracts when it hits the target and traps the prey very efficiently.

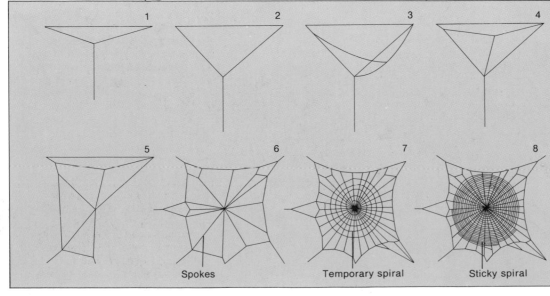

1　2　3　4

5　6　7　8

Spokes　Temporary spiral　Sticky spiral

Orb webs are the most familiar of spiders' traps. First, the spider makes a firmly anchored framework of strong, nonsticky silk. Spokelike lines are then made and held in position with a temporary, widely spaced spiral, later replaced with a closely spaced, sticky spiral.

The spider may wait at the center of the web or hide nearby, linked by a silk line which detects any disturbances near the web.

How do spiders use their silk?

The most important use of silk is to trap prey. Since spiders are generally short-sighted and can move fast for short distances only, they must make snares to ambush their victims. Once the prey has been trapped, a spider may swathe it in broad bands of silk, then bite it with its powerful jaws to inject paralyzing poison.

Although all spiders can produce silk from glands in their bodies, not all use it to make webs. The silk may be used as a safety line to anchor the spider as it moves about. It may also be made into a cocoon to protect the spider's eggs or a parachute to waft a baby spider into the air and to a new living place.

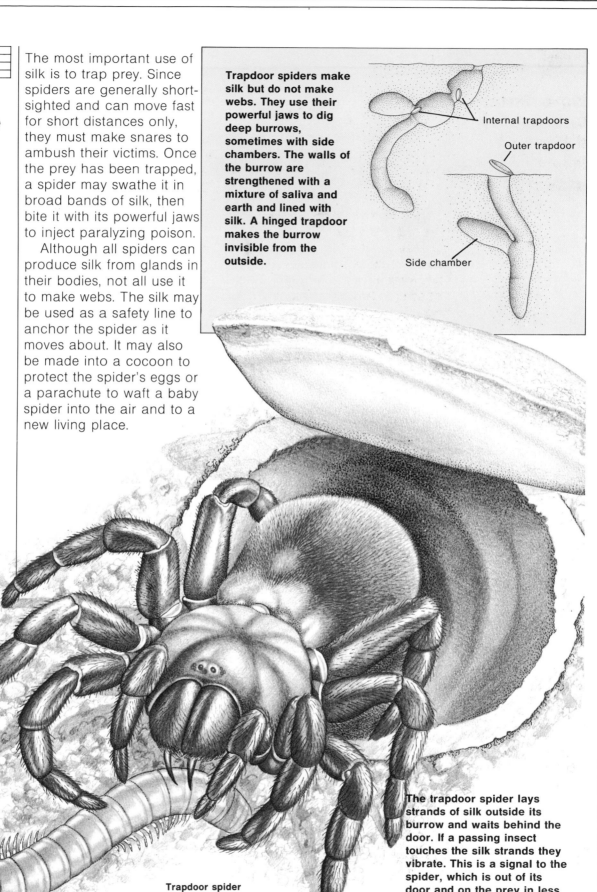

Trapdoor spiders make silk but do not make webs. They use their powerful jaws to dig deep burrows, sometimes with side chambers. The walls of the burrow are strengthened with a mixture of saliva and earth and lined with silk. A hinged trapdoor makes the burrow invisible from the outside.

Internal trapdoors

Outer trapdoor

Side chamber

Trapdoor spider

The trapdoor spider lays strands of silk outside its burrow and waits behind the door. If a passing insect touches the silk strands they vibrate. This is a signal to the spider, which is out of its door and on the prey in less than a second.

Do animals use tools?

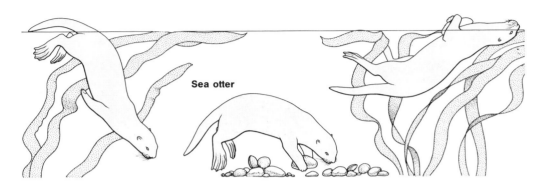

Sea otter

Many captive animals in zoos and circuses have been taught to use tools, usually to amuse mankind. In the wild just a few animals use tools of their own accord. They do so to get food which would not otherwise be available.

A tool is an object which the user takes from his surroundings and uses to make a task easier to perform. For example, a human being might use a penknife to cut things that teeth or fingernails could not manage. In the same way the Egyptian vulture uses a stone to crack open eggs which are too large for it to crush in its beak so would not normally be available as food. The sea otter, too, extends its diet by using a stone to crack open hard-shelled creatures.

Most of the few animals which do use some sort of tool can do so only for one specific activity, such as the examples mentioned; they cannot adapt their use of

Sea otters feed on prey such as mollusks, sea urchins and crabs, all of them armored with heavy shells. When the otter gathers its prey on the sea-bed it also collects a heavy flat pebble. While lying on its back on the water, the otter uses the stone as an anvil against which it smashes the shell of its meal.

tools to any other purpose. Only the apes seem able to use tools, such as sticks and stones, in different ways.

Because animals normally eat food that is readily and easily available, there is rarely any need for them to discover tools. Moreover, few animals can hold or handle objects—their limbs and hands are usually designed only for movement.

Making and using tools requires a high degree of brain power—more than most creatures possess. The ability of human beings to work out how to make and use tools sets us apart. Humans are even called "tool-making animals."

Woodpecker finch

The woodpecker finch of the Galapagos Islands feeds, like a true woodpecker, largely on grubs which burrow in the trunks of trees or stems of large cacti. It can detect the insects' tunnels but, since it does not have the woodpecker's long tongue, often cannot reach them. To solve the problem it picks up a cactus spine or a splinter of wood and uses it to bring the morsel within reach of its beak. As soon as the bird has caught its meal it drops this temporary tool.

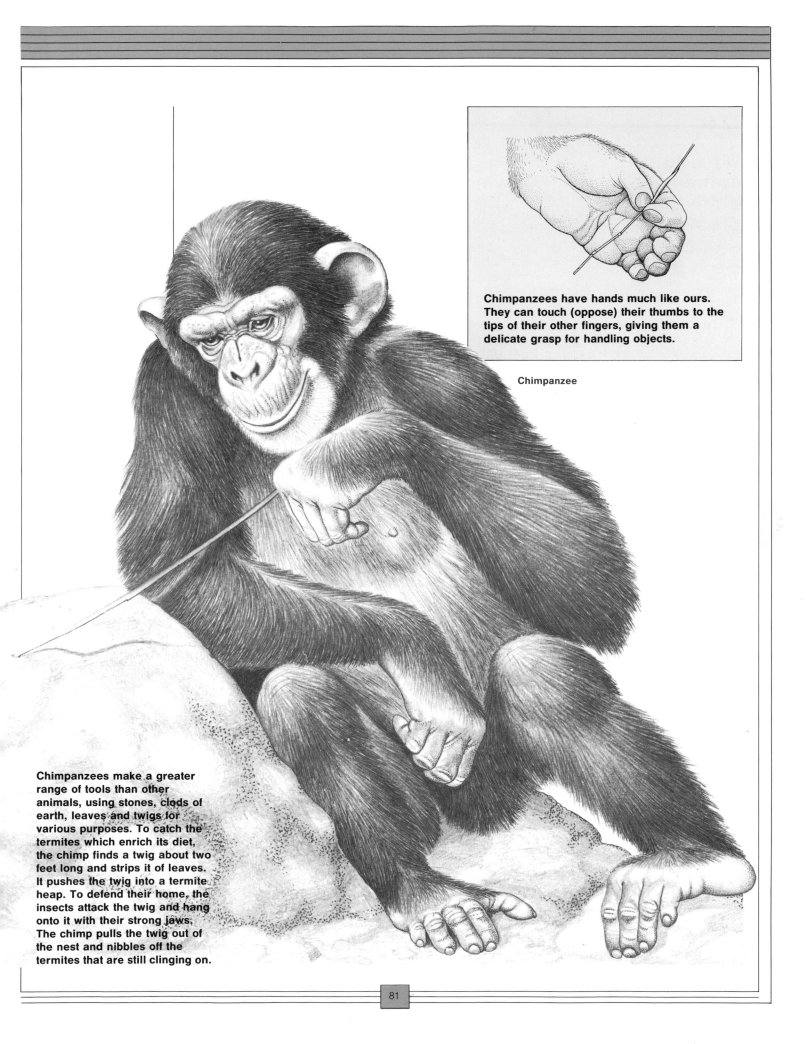

Chimpanzees have hands much like ours. They can touch (oppose) their thumbs to the tips of their other fingers, giving them a delicate grasp for handling objects.

Chimpanzee

Chimpanzees make a greater range of tools than other animals, using stones, clods of earth, leaves and twigs for various purposes. To catch the termites which enrich its diet, the chimp finds a twig about two feet long and strips it of leaves. It pushes the twig into a termite heap. To defend their home, the insects attack the twig and hang onto it with their strong jaws. The chimp pulls the twig out of the nest and nibbles off the termites that are still clinging on.

Why do some animals eat plants and some eat each other?

All animals have to eat some kind of food to provide their bodies with the fuel for life. Plants trap the sun's energy directly to make the food they need, but animals cannot do that. At best, they can obtain that energy secondhand by eating plants. A plant eater, or herbivore, is then available to be the food for another creature.

By eating the bodies of herbivores, the flesh eaters, or carnivores, still gain energy from the sun, the primary source, but they get it thirdhand. This transfer of energy can be thought of as a chain, leading from the plants, which are the first producers, through a series of links, each dependent on the one below it. The progression from one link to the next is not a simple one, since energy is used in different ways and only a small part is available to be passed on each time. For this reason, food chains are fairly short.

For the food chain to operate successfully there must always be a greater bulk of plants than of animals that feed on them and far more plant feeders than flesh eaters.

Such a chain can also be shown as a pyramid. The base is formed of the many and varied creatures which feed on plants while the upper levels are composed of ever smaller numbers of ever larger flesh eaters. The top of the pyramid contains the large animals, mainly carnivores such as lions and tigers, which are rarely, if ever, attacked and eaten by others. Sharks, eagles and crocodiles are usually top predators in their particular chains.

Because there are flesh eaters as well as plant feeders in the food chain, a greater number and variety of animals can survive in any area than if all of its inhabitants were feeding solely on plants.

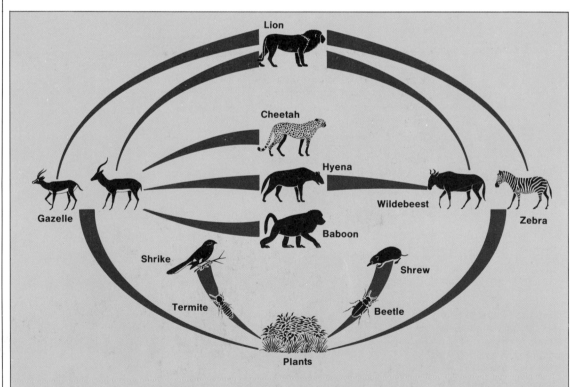

In the savannas of East Africa the grasses and shrubs provide food for many small animals such as beetles and termites as well as large ones such as antelopes and zebras. The small creatures are hunted by predators different from those which pursue larger prey. Insects, for example, are hunted by birds and small mammals while big cats and other carnivores hunt zebras and antelopes.

At the top of the chain is the lion, rarely attacked and eaten by other animals. The energy and minerals locked into its body are not released until after its death, when its body decomposes and returns to the earth.

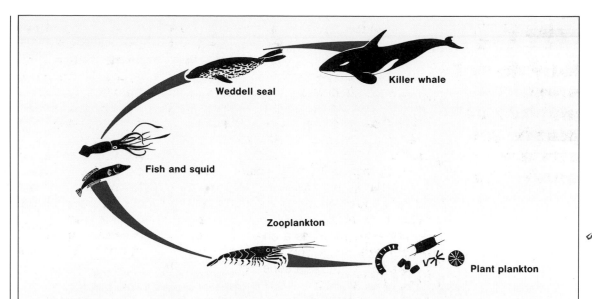

Weddell seal

Killer whale

Fish and squid

Zooplankton

Plant plankton

In the ocean microscopic plants (phytoplankton) are the primary food producers. They float in surface waters and are eaten by tiny animals, zooplankton. These in turn are food for creatures such as squid and fish, which are themselves eaten by seals and dolphins. The killer whale is a top predator, attacking large flesh eaters such as seals.

A herbivore needs to eat a greater weight of food each day in proportion to its body than a carnivore does, since plants are generally less nutritious than flesh. Most flesh eaters feed on animals considerably smaller than themselves, which they can kill quickly and easily. Social carnivores, such as lions and members of the dog family, may group together to attack and kill creatures much larger than themselves.

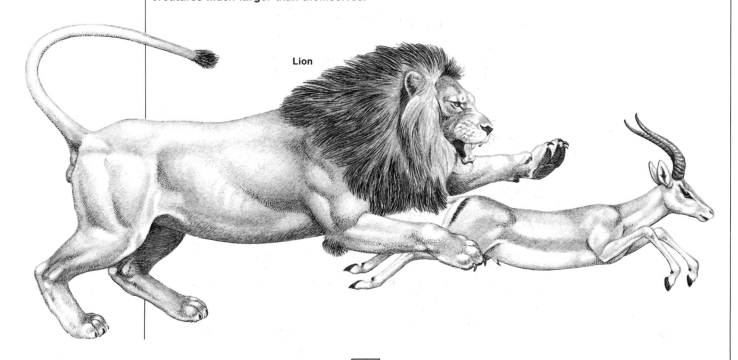

Lion

How do sea creatures catch their prey?

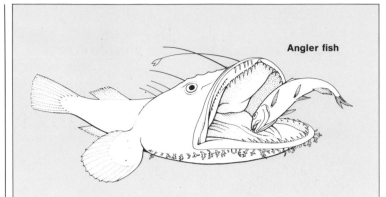

Angler fish

Almost all sharks are fast-swimming predators in the surface waters of tropical seas. The great white shark is one of the biggest at about 33 ft (10 m), and will feed on any large creatures it meets, including, occasionally, humans. More usual catches are big fish, seals and turtles. The shark detects its prey by sight, smell and the special lateral line sensory system possessed by most fish (see p 39). Once caught, the prey is sliced through by the shark's saw-edged teeth.

The angler fish is one of the many sea creatures that lies in wait for its prey, camouflaged by its flattened, irregular shape. It attracts prey by dangling a lure, formed from the first ray of its dorsal fin. When a creature approaches, mistaking the lure for a piece of food, the angler fish opens its mouth. Water rushes into the gaping jaws, taking with it the unfortunate prey. Other fish that ambush their prey are sting rays, which lie concealed in the sand or mud of the seabed, and stone fish, which hide among stones.

Marine hunters, like those on land, include creatures which chase their prey, some which ambush it and others which poison and paralyze it. Jellyfish and sea anemones, for example, may look too fragile to kill other animals for food, but they have an armory of poisonous sting cells on their tentacles.

Some fish, too, are inactive hunters. Many flatfish, including plaice and sole, spend their lives half-hidden on the sea-bed, catching any unwary creatures that come their way. Other fish are much more energetic in their searches. Mackerel, tuna and swordfish, for example, are efficient, fast-moving hunters.

Filter feeding is a means of gathering food which is unique to aquatic creatures. All the filter feeder needs to do is take in large amounts of water and pass it through some sort of sieving mechanism in its mouth or body. This sieve strains off tiny organisms, plants or animals, which live floating in the sea. Small animals such as sea squirts and clams filter feed, but so do many of the largest creatures in the sea. Rorquals and right whales, which are the biggest mammals, and the whale shark and basking shark, which are the biggest fish, are all filter feeders.

Great white shark

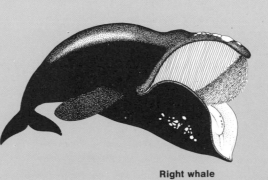

Filter feeders eat vast quantities of minute plants or animals which they strain from the water. The tiny sea squirt— about 3 in (7.5 cm) long—just stays in one place pumping water through its body. Food items are strained out in a special filter region. At the other extreme is the huge right whale, about 50 ft (15.2 m) long. Like all filter-feeding whales it has a fringe of huge, brushlike plates in its mouth. As the whale swims slowly along with its mouth open, these plates catch any suitable food items, mainly the tiny shrimplike crustaceans known as krill.

Right whale

Sea squirt

How do birds catch their prey?

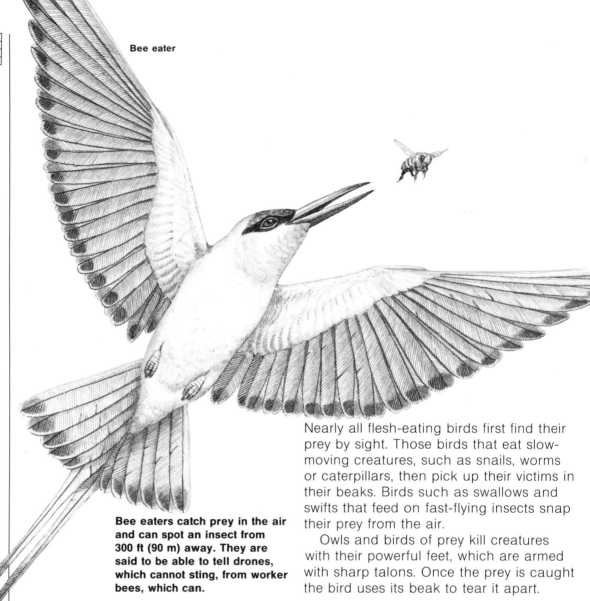

Bee eater

Bee eaters catch prey in the air and can spot an insect from 300 ft (90 m) away. They are said to be able to tell drones, which cannot sting, from worker bees, which can.

Nearly all flesh-eating birds first find their prey by sight. Those birds that eat slow-moving creatures, such as snails, worms or caterpillars, then pick up their victims in their beaks. Birds such as swallows and swifts that feed on fast-flying insects snap their prey from the air.

Owls and birds of prey kill creatures with their powerful feet, which are armed with sharp talons. Once the prey is caught the bird uses its beak to tear it apart.

From as high as 100 ft (30 m) above the sea, the gannet sights its prey. Folding its wings back against its body, it plummets into the water to just below where the fish is swimming. As the gannet rises to the surface it seizes the fish in its long sharp beak. No diving bird actually spears fish since this would hold its beak shut.

Gannet

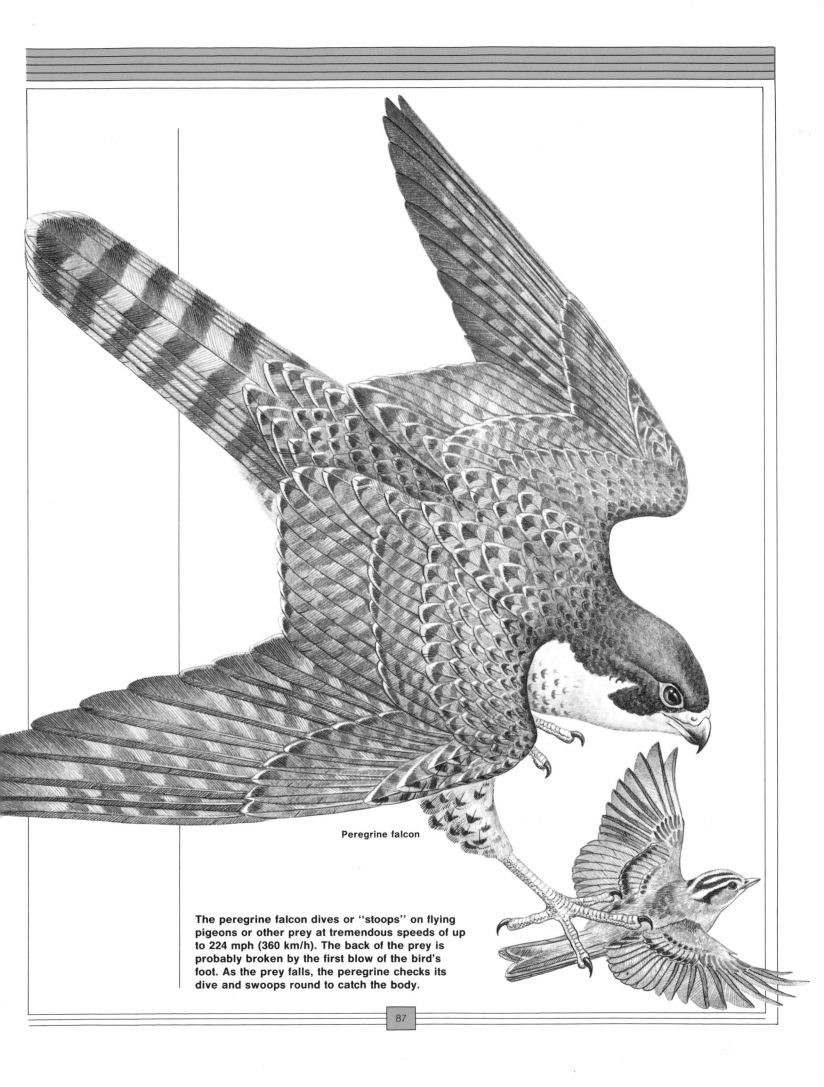

Peregrine falcon

The peregrine falcon dives or "stoops" on flying pigeons or other prey at tremendous speeds of up to 224 mph (360 km/h). The back of the prey is probably broken by the first blow of the bird's foot. As the prey falls, the peregrine checks its dive and swoops round to catch the body.

79

Which is the most poisonous snake?

The most poisonous of all snakes is thought to be the black-headed sea snake. When tested in a laboratory for its ability to kill mice, its venom proved to be about one hundred times as toxic as that of any other known snake. Fortunately, this snake generally reserves its poison for the small eels on which it feeds.

Sea snakes have small heads and can deliver only small amounts of poison. Other snakes, such as some cobras and vipers, deliver much more venom at a time. The Gabon viper, for example, may produce nearly a gram (0.03 oz).

A poisonous snake uses venom to subdue its prey and to start the

digestion of its flesh. The first of these processes is achieved by compounds which act on the nervous system, the second by substances which break down protein. All snake venom contains both components, but the proportions vary. The snake venom most dangerous to man contains a large percentage of the nerve poison, since this may act before any treatment can begin.

Human reactions to snake bites vary. The poison of the saw-scaled viper, a common and aggressive snake found from North Africa to Sri Lanka, is so toxic to man that the tiniest dose is lethal. Other very poisonous snakes include the Asian kraits and the North American coral snake.

80

Which is the largest snake?

The longest poisonous snake is the king cobra or hamadryad which may grow to more than 18 ft (5.5 m). But this is a slender snake and the heaviest poisonous snake is the eastern diamondback rattlesnake which may weigh as much as 34 lb (15.4 kg).

It is difficult to measure living snakes and many records are exaggerated. But it

is certain that constricting species, such as pythons, are far larger than venomous snakes. The reticulated python is thought to be the species with greatest average length—one specimen shot was 32 ft 2 ins (9.75 m). The anaconda, however, is the heaviest living snake; a 30 ft (9 m) specimen can be twice the weight of a reticulated python of the same length.

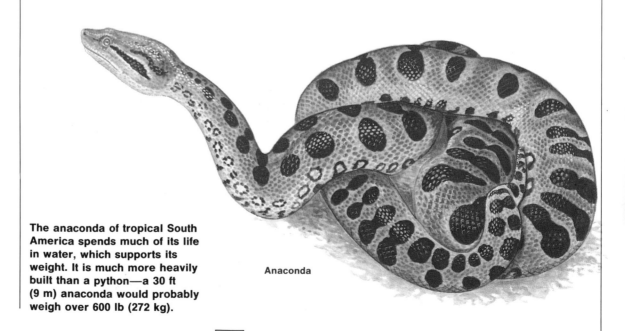

The anaconda of tropical South America spends much of its life in water, which supports its weight. It is much more heavily built than a python—a 30 ft (9 m) anaconda would probably weigh over 600 lb (272 kg).

Anaconda

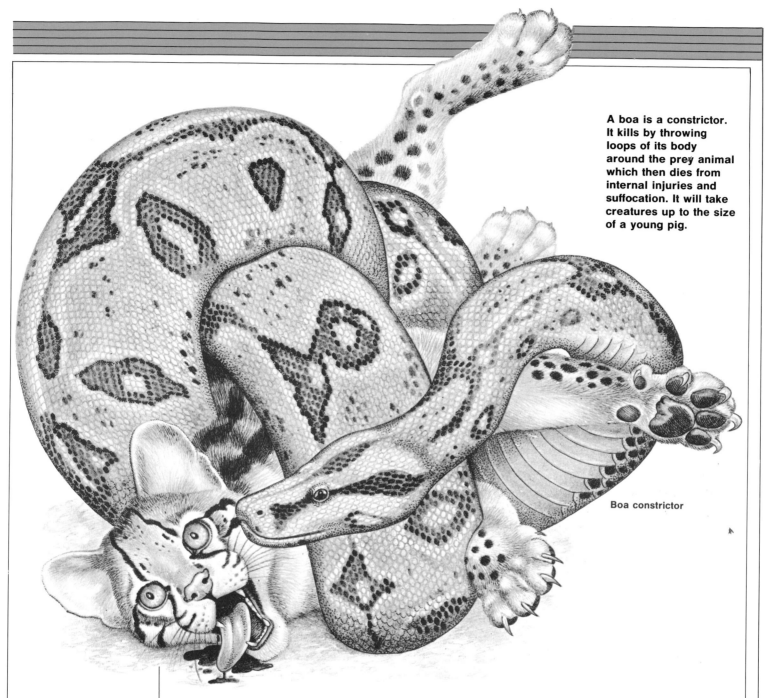

A boa is a constrictor. It kills by throwing loops of its body around the prey animal which then dies from internal injuries and suffocation. It will take creatures up to the size of a young pig.

Boa constrictor

81

How do snakes kill their prey?

About a third of all snakes kill their prey by venom. In these snakes the salivary glands at the back of the jaw have become modified into poison producers. In some species the venom runs down teeth near the back of the jaw; in others it is channeled on either side of the jaw to a large fang so that it is injected into the wound as the snake bites.

All the largest species of snakes are constrictors—they suffocate their prey with the strong coils of their own bodies. Other snakes merely grasp and swallow prey. All snakes have flexible jaws which separate in the middle. This allows a snake to engulf a meal with a larger circumference than its own body.

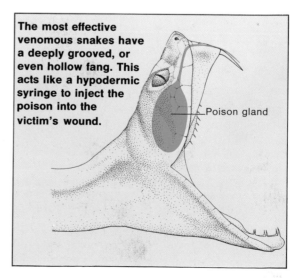

The most effective venomous snakes have a deeply grooved, or even hollow fang. This acts like a hypodermic syringe to inject the poison into the victim's wound.

Poison gland

Common vampire bat

Do vampire bats really eat blood?

Vampire bats do feed on blood. While all animals that feed on the flesh of others consume some, blood is the sole diet of these bats.

Vampire bats, which live in the southern United States and the forests of Central and South America, sleep during the day and fly out at night to find food. The bat lands near its prey, often a large mammal such as a horse or cow, and climbs up onto it to feed. Since blood contains a good deal of water, the bat may need to eat over its own weight in a single meal to obtain enough food. Most prey animals suffer little from one attack, but vampires may feed time after time on farm stock, which cannot escape, and take a great deal of blood from them.

Vampires may also infect their prey with rabies. Studies carried out in Trinidad show that one vampire in every 200 carries this disease.

Using its sharp incisor teeth, the bat makes a shallow cut in its victim's skin, slicing through tiny blood vessels. The wound bleeds profusely— substances in the bat's saliva stop the blood clotting easily—and the bat laps up its meal.

What do other bats eat?

Long-tongued bat

A nectar-feeding bat may have a tongue that, when protruded, is longer than the animal's head. With such a tongue, the bat can reach the nectar held deep inside the bell-like form of many tropical flowers. Most nectar feeders have small weak teeth, since they do not need to chew their liquid food.

Most of the 900 or more kinds of bat in the world feed on insects which they catch in flight using their system of animal sonar (see p 12). A few eat larger prey, including birds and small mammals, even other kinds of bat. Others eat fish which they detect near the surface of the water, using their sonar, and catch with their hind feet.

Many other bats are vegetarians, some feeding on fruit, others on nectar. The nectar-feeding bats have tongues which are fringed at the tips. When the bat plunges its brushlike tongue into a flower it absorbs the liquid sugars. As it feeds, the bat may get pollen on its chin and neck which is then passed on to the next flower that it visits. In this way bats pollinate many tropical plants.

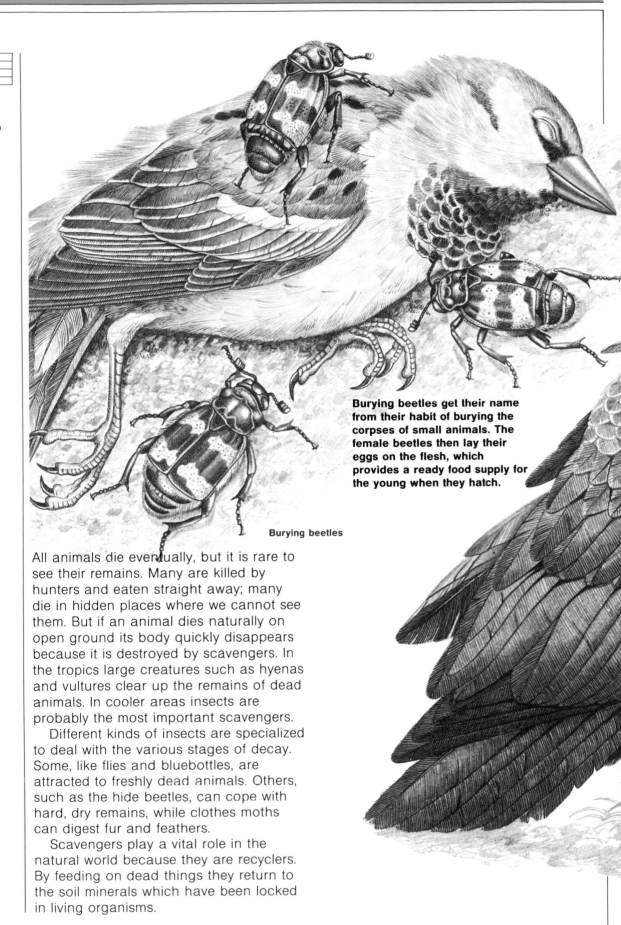

What happens to animals when they die?

Burying beetles get their name from their habit of burying the corpses of small animals. The female beetles then lay their eggs on the flesh, which provides a ready food supply for the young when they hatch.

Burying beetles

All animals die eventually, but it is rare to see their remains. Many are killed by hunters and eaten straight away; many die in hidden places where we cannot see them. But if an animal dies naturally on open ground its body quickly disappears because it is destroyed by scavengers. In the tropics large creatures such as hyenas and vultures clear up the remains of dead animals. In cooler areas insects are probably the most important scavengers.

Different kinds of insects are specialized to deal with the various stages of decay. Some, like flies and bluebottles, are attracted to freshly dead animals. Others, such as the hide beetles, can cope with hard, dry remains, while clothes moths can digest fur and feathers.

Scavengers play a vital role in the natural world because they are recyclers. By feeding on dead things they return to the soil minerals which have been locked in living organisms.

How do scavengers find their food?

Vultures are the master scavengers among the birds. Experiments have shown that most kinds rely totally on sight to find their food—like almost all birds they have virtually no sense of smell.

Each vulture soars in a large circle, scanning the ground below. If a dead or dying animal is spotted, the nearest vulture drops to the ground to investigate. Its descent is spotted by vultures in neighboring circles of the sky and they drift over to check the reason. Like ripples on a pool, their activity alerts birds still farther away which also fly in. Within minutes a freshly dead corpse has its congregation of scavengers.

White-backed vulture

Vultures usually have bare skin on their heads, not feathers. This is because, as scavengers, they often thrust their heads deep into the decaying flesh or body cavity of a dead animal. Head feathers would become clotted and soiled with blood, so the birds remain cleaner without them.

White-headed vulture

Index

Page numbers in italics indicate illustrations.